MALA & THE MASK OF GOLD

MALA
&
THE MASK
OF GOLD

JAIME MARTIN KO ATILANO

NEW DEGREE PRESS

MALA & THE MASK OF GOLD

ISBN   978-1-63676-562-4 *Paperback*

978-1-63676-146-6 *Kindle Ebook*

978-1-63676-147-3 *Ebook*

To my Mom, Tito Robert, Patrick, and Daniel,
thank you for fighting for my dreams.

To my extended family, dear friends, and the hometown homies,
I hope you get lost in this dream.

To the boy who was the moon, and I followed the moonlight,
mahal kita, Meek.

To the LGBTQ+ community, my people of Zamboanga City
and the Philippines, and for those who just want
a new adventure to read, this book is for you.

CONTENTS

———

"Always remember, embracing life's ambiguity can help shape you into the person you are destined to be."

—BY JAIME MARTIN KO ATILANO

A NOTE FROM
THE AUTHOR

Adventure and identity play hand in hand. We establish our identities based on our unique experiences within this world. I learned and gained these inspirations of storytelling from many great works of fiction. One example is *The Adventures of Huckleberry Finn* by Mark Twain. Twain's approach to writing is a compelling combination of adventure-story and identity -based themes within his protagonists. Through adventure, I wanted to share reflections of my own similar experiences as a queer Filipinx author. These are present in the adventures of Mala and Salem as they explore the magical fantasy of their world, one which is largely inspired by the mythology and spiritual aspects of the Tagalog Islands.

As a genderfluid individual, I had a difficult time finding ways to relate with modern stories and books. Due to this disconnect and lack of representation, I found a different way to deal with my internal struggles about my identity outside of reading some of my favorite works of fiction. I was exposed to LGBTQ+ literature in college, through the critical works of

James Baldwin, Audre Lorde, Oscar Wilde, and Leslie Feinberg, to name a few. I saw, even within these works, a need to address this diversity gap in LGBTQ+ representation.

For me, gender identity and sexuality has always been an exploration—an adventure. The process of finding myself and fighting my fears was never a light switch moment. In hindsight, I realized that I processed different moments at different stages and experiences in my life in many different ways. When I stopped thinking about my gender and sexuality as an on-off switch and embraced the journey and adventure, I suddenly began to find myself. I realized that coming out is a never-ending process, like a revolving door that never closes. For example, I came out as gay in my junior year of high school, but later in life, while in college, I recame out as genderfluid. Once I got to know myself more, I realized there was more to my identity than I could have ever imagined. I would have to come out again to different people as I arrived at new spaces like working in a new job or meeting new people. I even needed to explain genderfluidity to old friends and close relatives because my identity is one with which they were not familiar at all. The importance of growth became a telling theme throughout my process of coming out. I found power in accepting how I am different and learned not to view my genderfluidity as something of which to be afraid. Accepting difference can be a source of strength.

In this book, I attempt to show this power through Mala's character—the genderfluid protagonist. Mala's experience as a genderfluid character is not at all meant to represent the entire LGBTQ+ community or to stand as a thorough example for those who may identify as genderfluid. Mala, instead, is meant to be a celebration of non-binary and genderfluid identity that also existed in the pre-colonial Filipinx past. *Mala & the Mask of Gold* approaches the role of gender within the pre-colonial Philippine societies, examining how masculinity and femininity played huge roles in social function, yet also allowed the qualities and attributes often assigned to masculinity and femininity to be more fluid and accepted amongst members of the community.

We see these fluidities play out in a variety of ways, from the existence of warrior women leaders and the significant roles of women shamans, to the acknowledgement that some of these roles included transgender (trans) women. It is important to note that the context of transgender, non-binary, or genderfluid were discursively created and were not terms used during the pre-colonial Philippine times.

My identity as a Filipinx immigrant is hugely important, as well. I was born in Zamboanga City, Philippines, off the southern islands of Mindanao. I came as an immigrant to America around the age of nine, and I have always valued my culture and traditions. They make me who I am today. I grew up without my mother, as she worked to support a life, here in America, for my older brother and me. It took several years for us to finally find one another. Growing up without a mother at a young age was difficult, but I will always cherish and admire her sacrifices and struggles to give us a better life here in the US.

I especially want to highlight and celebrate the Filipino/a/x community as my people and my culture are aspects of my identity that are very dear to me. I don't want our history and mythology from pre-colonization to be erased. *The Aswang Project* is an educational resource that shares the rich and diverse mythology and folklore of the Philippines with a wide audience. This has been a huge resource in my research and exploration of Philippine history and discovery of how trade within Southeast Asia and Colonization from the Spanish affected our folklore and mythology. A member of *The Aswang Project* told me, "I think presenting Philippine mythology in your work is the best way to support the spread of knowledge and interest in the subject. I'm glad you've taken it on." I wanted to keep my people's history and my people's story alive within this work.

This story is meant to be somewhat of a love letter to my communities; a story of strength and hope for the LGBTQ+ community and for young readers and young-adult readers who may deal with the adversities of being different. If you are exploring the challenges of being genderqueer, having to provide for the family at a young age, or battling inner monsters to find your power and purpose in this world, *Mala & the Mask of Gold* is for you.

With that being said, I truly hope you enjoy reading this book.

Note: This is purely a work of fiction but is inspired by a rich and wonderful culture.

Art by Kayla Creavalle

CHAPTER 1

THE *AKLATAN*

Mala

I wake up and realize I am not in my room. I look around to find myself in a garden surrounded by lilacs, vibrant with purple hues. The stars cast a white glow on everything they touch. Getting up, I felt a slight breeze blow across my body, my black hair wisping into the chilling air as the flower petals dance in the sky.

"This isn't real," I think to myself.

Yet, I still feel the wind brush against my skin. I smell a strong, sweet, heady scent with hints of vanilla. I still see the silver light glow in the dark blue and purple hue of the sky. The garden seems endless as I stare into the horizon. This, I think again, must be a dream.

A butterfly passes, its long tail fluttering beautifully, like the waves of the ocean of my home. Its black and white stripes contrast with the mauve hues of the valley of flowers. I follow it.

Forward I go, my eyes focused solely on the butterfly's wings. Like a kite, it glides in the air, guiding me to its mystery destination.

The butterfly flutters and lands on a mirror standing upright in the middle of the field. The length of this mirror matches my height, its sides seemingly made of white marble. It has shapes of the butterfly wings attached to it—one forewing on each side. A long tail extends behind the mirror. I walk slowly to see my reflection, but I do not see myself—instead, I meet eyes with a woman wearing a golden mask. I do not recognize the woman behind the mask, but she feels familiar and her warm energy radiates outside of the mirror. The chill of the garden leaves as I take in her heat. *Have I met this woman before?*

Her eyes are striking, even behind the mask. They burn, a great golden hazel, like stars in the night—different from my own dark brown eyes. Above her head sits a pristine crown with pink, ruby-like encrusted jewels. Her long, white, silky hair almost touches the tips of her feet.

Her feminine presence is divine, but a strong masculine energy also radiates from her reflection. She is powerful and I can feel her headstrong aura. This energy reminds me of the commanding warrior spirit, much like my *Kuya,*[1] Salem. The woman in the mask is tall and slender, but also carries strong, masculine shoulders.

What intrigues me is her outfit, how it sits charmingly on her silver skin. She wears a beautiful lavender-lace gown, with a golden royal tunic layered on top of it. I have never seen attire like this before, tender yet strapping. The being herself is beautiful, nonetheless. I look up to see the person in the reflection staring back, her deep hazel eyes sparkling.

I slowly raise my right hand toward the mirror. The woman raises her hand back. As I reach out, so does she,

---

1   Kuya – Older Brother

and our palms connect on the glass surface. I feel the warm softness of the woman's mystical touch; her energy flows right through me as if the glass that separates us holds no matter. *Can she feel mine, too–my energy?* I think.

"*Ate?*"[2] says a voice.

Before I can look behind myself to discover the speaker, I wake up.

"Wake up, little brother!" howls Salem.

This sound is like hearing the crow of the rooster, and I wake from my slumber. My head and body feel heavy, as if they have been ripped away and dragged back into this reality. My dreams have never made me feel this groggy and drained. This dream feels so special, it has to mean something. I remember the dream, everything about it, so vividly. It feels as though it had been real. Disgruntled, I step out of bed to see my older brother in my room. His tall and earnest manner hangs over above me, holding a bowl of rice with cooked fish on top. Salem always provides me with food. His hunts are his greatest prize and cooking them is how he savors his talents of catching game.

"Eat up," he says proudly, and I, of course, oblige.

I am so tired from the morning's dream, but eating my brother's cooking slowly revives me. I always appreciate his generosity.

"You're the best, *Kuya*!" I say, smiling weakly.

"You look really tired, Mala. Up late last night?" he asks.

---

2   Ate (ah-teh) – Older Sister

Should I tell Salem? I know he is worried for my health. Maybe Kuya would have an explanation. He is always so logical, and I rely on him whenever I need help. *But would he even believe me, though? I mean, it was just a dream after all. And who was that woman in the mirror, and who called out my name?*

As I continue to eat my bowl, lost in my own thoughts, Salem rubs the top of my head playfully with his fist. I decide not to tell him yet. *Not until I know what is going on.* He begins packing up his sword and arrows, preparing to exit.

"Well, no worries, I know my food will help make you feel better. I have to leave now to prepare for some things for the final ceremony. Tomorrow's the day, Mala."

That's right, tomorrow is the day Salem will finally be initiated to become a warrior. But not just any warrior—a Blood Moon Knight, a title bestowed upon those who sacrifice their life for the Great Deity of the Lunar Eclipse, *Bakunawa.*[3] This title is nothing more than a title of pain. I had always held disdain toward the Blood Moon Knights and their ways, especially because they took our own father from us. Warriors always choose duty over other important things like family. I can't understand Salem's reasoning to become a Blood Moon Knight. *Does Kuya really want to be like our father?*

"Does Father know? Will he be attending the initiation, too?" I ask.

"No," he responds sharply, "That man is always busy. What does it have to do with him?"

I can tell I have struck a sensitive nerve. Father never shows up. Not when it matters.

---

3   Bakunawa – Deity of Eclipses; Creator of the Lunar Eclipse; The Great Serpent; Worshipped by the Blood Moon Knights

"You're right, I'm sorry I asked. I wish I could be there, but I know only recognized Blood Moon Knights are allowed. I'm proud of you, *Kuya*," I say. I want to support my brother, even if I don't support him becoming a Blood Moon Knight.

"No worries, little brother, I know you will be with me in spirit. *Salamat*," he says.[4] He waves goodbye and exits my room. I hear his loud, sturdy steps as he heads down the stairs and closes the door from outside. I can tell he needs to be alone, likely because I mentioned Father at a time where he should be celebrating an achievement.

Alone, I cannot help but continue to think about my dream. I recall the Mask of Gold that concealed the woman's identity, how glamorously it shined. It must have been a clue. *What does it all mean? Where can I go to find some answers?*

I process my thoughts carefully, allowing the silence of the room to ease me into my own mind. Then, it hits me. *The Aklatan!* There is no other place to find answers than my favorite in the city.

Whenever I wander in thought, I go to the *Aklatan*—a large hall that archives readings, documents, and scriptures in the City of *Zambo*. Maybe I can find an answer about my dream there, or readings on a Mask of Gold. I finish my meal and head downstairs. Outside the kitchen door, there is an opening into the forest.

I follow the trail into the trees and walk until I reach the city. The sun's morning glare shines in-between the leaves of the trees. I like the feeling of the sun; its warm embrace fills me with life and energy. The heat of the summer's humidity makes me sweat.

---

4   Salamat – Thank you

Energy has always been something that I can feel strongly, ever since I was young. I can feel the energy of nature, of animals living their lives. Sometimes I believe I hear plants singing melodies, as if the earth is conducting a symphony and harmonizing with the rivers and trees around me. I have always felt safe, here, in the forest. The trail leads me into the outskirts of the city.

The City of *Zambo* is home to the fishing waters at the southern peninsula of the island. There, a lively market lines the outskirts of the city near the ship port. The animated traders by the sandy beaches bring a surge of energy and excitement to my spirit. The market is full of citizens, merchants, buyers, and families, all crowding the street. The sounds of bargaining, eating, and laughter fill the air. The energies of people are much different than that of the plants, earth, and animals of the forest. People are generally noisy; their energy does not sound like songs but like vibrations dancing rhythmically in the air. One might think it overwhelming, but I generally enjoy the liveliness of it all from time to time, although I much prefer the slow energies produced in the halls of the *Aklatan*.

Freshly caught fish and seafood reek in the air as the fishermen of *Zambo* pass by. The fishermen are mostly topless and wear headbands and loincloths, returning from a day at sea. Salem will sometimes sell his catches here, alongside the fishermen, and will find the best deals on trade for meat, rice, and clothing.

Not one moment into the city, traders from all over try to sell their pieces of clothing and jewelry to me as I walk the wet, cold-stone roads through the market. I am curious and intrigued by the beautiful craft and creations of the traders. So many of them are not just hunters, but artists, painters, craftspeople, too.

"Bucket of clams for you, miss?" asks a man. *Miss.* Another person who also recognizes me as a *miss.* A simple honorific, but also a powerful word that usually addresses a woman. *Am I a woman?* Sometimes, I feel that way, noticing the strong feminine energy within me. I have always grown up feeling like a *miss* at times and at other times, also *not a miss.* This feeling—it is not like a tug of war between my identity, but instead like a shifting of the soul.

"No! Don't waste your coin on those catches, come see this beautiful necklace that will look so good on you, child!" another trader interrupts.

"No, thank you!" I smile at the traders as I hastily move through the overcrowded market.

I take a moment to observe the busy environment and feel the vibrations of people through the air until I notice a group of young girls around my age looking at a piece of pearl jewelry. The girls give off similar waves of energy that I sense within myself, delicate, yet vibrant and upbeat. I too love pearls, and it leads me to touch the pearl necklace around my neck, given to me by my mother. I never had the chance to meet my mother, as she had died giving birth to me, but the pearl necklace connects me to her spirit, as if she is always with me, watching over my life.

One of girls in the group notices my stares. Surprised, I quickly wave to say hello. *Maybe this time will be different,* I think to myself. I want to talk about pearls with them and yearn to have that sisterly bond that they have between them, but then one girl suddenly whispers something to the group. The girls mockingly laugh at me and leave the shopkeeper's selling stand. Once they see me, I can always feel the girls' energy change. The sudden shift in the vibration of their spirits makes me cringe. I sense the waves change from gentle to malicious. I can tell the girls are confused and fearful, as if I am haunted, despite my own feelings of hurt. *Is it the way I look?* I ask myself. And then I hear it, the whisper of "monster" under their sly breaths as they hide away from me. *Am I a monster to them?* Although I feel sad and hurt, these feelings are not new to me, so I move on through the market.

From a young age, I realized each living person had their own unique aura close to them. This aura projects their feelings in vibrations, the same way plants, earth, and animals grow, shift, and make sounds. These vibrations are the songs of each person's soul and the waves they emit are how they interact with the world around them. At least, that's what I like to believe. I could always feel it, and growing up, it was something with which I learned to cope, but I wish I could meet others who feel this energy, too. It's what makes me feel alone and separated from the rest of the citizens of *Zambo*, like a ghost in a crowd, separated from the physical realm.

Although my gender is free, I don't always feel free in my body. The way the people treat me makes me feel like a prisoner in my home. It hurts, but it is a pain to which I have grown numb over the years.

I want to leave the market and hide myself away into the halls of the *Aklatan*, so I do. Out of the market and into the depths of the city, I arrive at the *Aklatan*'s grand entrance. Each time I arrive, I am always mesmerized by the beautifully carved stone that lines the outside of the building. The wooden doors are held by black steel hinges. The *Aklatan* always makes me feel less alone. This place is like a second home for me–a sanctuary. I don't have friends—not in the city or at home. So, I find solace in the stories of books and readings. Reading stories of fantasy and folklore has become my escape. With stories, I don't have to worry about the pain of rejection from people. I have only ever really had Salem, but he is always busy hunting or training,

Something about a Mask of Gold has to be in here.

I go inside and am immediately struck by the strong whiff of the wood, the old papyrus filling the air as I observe the collection of old books, scrolls, and documents. The archives, the collection of readings inside the *Aklatan*, are a large, curated collection of stories and texts. The *Aklatan* is a significant and important place of knowledge in *Zambo*. Scholars, warriors, and even merchants visit this place to learn more and to trade information and documentation.

Most of the readings that reside on the shelves are about the quests of the Blood Moon Knights. In these stories, the warriors are seen as heroes, succeeding in their adventures all in the name of *Bakunawa*. There are also stories of the people of *Zambo* who lived and served under the great warriors and were made to believe in the *Bakunawa*, too. There are, however, no stories about the Great *Bakunawa*. She remains a mystery, an unknown enigma. Her power is to be feared. If we, the people, ever disobey, we will be punished. I always try to find other readings, some that do not pertain to these quests if I have the time. Thankfully, the archives are large enough to hold many other stories and tales that I can enjoy.

"Mala, a pleasure to see you back again! More books about *Engkantos* today?"[5] says a sudden, rusted voice from behind me.

"Keeper *Alma*! Hello to you, too! No, unfortunately, not today. I'm looking for a specific kind of book, actually."

---

5   Engkantos - Fairies or mythical spirits

His old, tired face musters a gentle and sweet smile. He wears the usual *barong*[6] and he slowly walks over to me, "Please, *Anak*,[7] how many times do I need to tell you, call me your *Lolo Alma*,"[8] he fixes his weary glasses, "and always happy to help you, a regular of the *Aklatan*."

I smile and chuckle at the thought. Maybe I don't have friends around my age, but I am grateful for my relationship with *Lolo Alma*, who treats me like I am his own grandchild. He is the keeper of the *Aklatan*, and one of the smartest citizens of *Zambo*. He has lived most of his life here in the *Aklatan*, preserving all he can about the powerful information and history of our people and city.

"Does the *Aklatan* have any stories or information about a Mask of Gold? Anything magical?"

"Mask of Gold, hmmm…" he takes a moment to think as he rubs his long, charcoal-stained beard. "We do have many documents about the cultural significance of masks, but nothing particular to golden masks. But now that I think of it, we did procure new shipment of texts today from the Blood Moon Knights' recent raid. I can refer you to them if you like!"

"No, *Lolo Alma*, it's okay. I don't think those texts will help." I also don't want to read anything taken from a raid. Those stories belong to others and it feels wrong that they are stolen and kept here. *I wonder if many of the books I read are from raids.*

"May I ask why you are looking into stories about a magical golden mask, *Anak*?"

---

6   Barong - Embroidered long sleeved traditional garment
7   Anak - Child
8   Lolo - Grandfather; Elder

I look both ways to make sure no one is listening. My suspicious gazing around puzzles *Lolo Alma*, his face full of concern.

I whisper, "Okay keep this a secret between you and me. *Lolo*, I had a dream. It was a really weird dream about waking up in a garden of purple flowers. I looked into this mirror that was in the middle of the garden and there was this woman! She was glowing silver and wearing this beautiful Mask of Gold. I just feel like I have to find out more."

Lolo nods his head, closing his eyes, "Hmmm! Sounds like you were dealing with some sort of spiritual dream. I would refer you to a *Babaylan* to decipher, but sadly, we don't have any *Babaylans* here in *Zambo*...not anymore."

"*Babaylan*?[9] What is that *Lolo Alma*?"

"It's not a what, *Anak*, but a whom," he corrects. "*Babaylans* are known as shamans—spiritual practitioners, to be exact. One would be able to help decipher these visions in your dreams."

"Wow! That's amazing. Why have I never heard of them before?"

"You've never heard of them because we lost our only *Babaylan* in *Zambo* during the invasion of the Blood Moon Knights. This was before your time. Her name was Lau. She was a dear friend of mine when I was much younger." His graceful smile slowly fades into a depressing frown. The air begins to feel heavy.

"I'm so sorry to hear of your loss, *Lolo*," I say. I touch my necklace again. I understand the pain of losing someone early in life, but to lose a friend, especially from an invasion

---

9   Babaylan – Shaman; spiritual practitioners of the pre-colonial Philippine islands

of warriors that we commemorate today, must be so hard for *Lolo Alma*. I had not known the Blood Moon Knights had invaded our very own island.

"It is nice to remember my old friend, even to speak of her again, no matter how sad. She would have liked you for sure," he assures me. "Many of her old *Babaylan* scriptures were burned by the Blood Moon Knights, as they believed it to be witchcraft and against the beliefs of the *Bakunawa*."

Lolo Alma glances over his shoulder and whispers, "But I was able to save a copperplate inscription that they were unable to burn. It was my last memento of her. Maybe the answer to your dreams lies somewhere in the text."

My eyes widen. *A clue!*

"Really, *Lolo*, you would entrust me with such a scripture?"

Lolo Alma nods, "I couldn't read it even if I tried. It's written in ancient *Baybayin*[10] script and throughout all my years here in the *Aklatan*, I was never lucky enough to find a scholar to translate the old text. *Babaylans* were trained to read the old writing system, and they would document spell rituals and notes in their scrolls. It'll do more good for you than for me, but you'll have to find someone who can translate it for you. Come follow me, *Anak*."

Lolo Alma leads me down a narrow pathway toward a door. Inside the door is a small room. *Lolo* pulls one of the books off the shelf, and it opens a hidden corridor. I am amazed at how large and mysterious the *Aklatan* remains. It has rooms within rooms that only the keeper knows. "This way," he says, and I follow.

Down the secret corridor is a staircase that leads down deeper within the chambers of the *Aklatan*. *Lolo Alma* grabs

---

10   Baybayin – Ancient writing script of the pre-colonial Philippines

a torch, flaming from inside the top of the steps, and starts walking down until we reach a much larger room—a chamber beneath the archives of the building. "Welcome to my home." he says.

The room is vast. I can see the bed in which *Lolo Alma* sleeps at night and a huge wooden table in the middle of the room. Books, papers, and notes are scattered across the room, contrasting the neatly stocked documents above the chamber.

"My apologies for the mess. My research can get a bit messy. I take care of the archives more than I do my own living space, as you can tell."

"Wow! *Lolo*, you really live down here in a secret room?"

Lolo chuckles, "Not so secret, but it is my personal domain. Even the Blood Moon Knights are not allowed to enter these premises. As a Keeper, I was awarded this privilege to make a home within the *Aklatan*. My days and nights are conducted here, in this place of knowledge. It is my duty to protect our collection at all times. I could never leave, even if it were my will to do so."

I notice a chest lying in the back of the room. *Lolo Alma* grabs a key from his side pocket and inserts it into the keyhole. With one twist, a loud clink sounds around the room as he opens the chest. Suddenly, I feel a wave of energy rush throughout my body, as if what lay inside the chest was calling to me. He pulls out the copperplate tablet from inside, its reflection shines in the light. He sets it on the table, and I rush over to see it.

"This copperplate inscription is one of the earliest written documents found in our history. My dear friend held it close for years, protecting this magnificent scripture, and now it is yours to keep."

I see the inscription of the text, the symbols unrecognizable, but a distinct beauty to the writing. *Could this really hold the answers to my dream?* I lightly touch the copperplate, feeling the indented symbols and patterns with the tips of my fingers.

"You see, it was believed that *Baybayin* are the writings and words of not only mankind, but of the deities, too. It's how my old friend used to communicate with spirits and deities during her spiritual practices. I never had the chance to learn the old writings myself," *Lolo Alma* notes.

Oddly, these symbols feel familiar to me. Suddenly, I sense a second wave of energy flow inside my body. The vibrations of the energy feel like a large anchor being lifted from inside of me. With one large exhale of air, my insides become light as a feather. I feel unlocked. My mind becomes clear and open as the symbols formulate into letters in my head. Those letters transform to meanings, as if this inscription were meant to be found by me, just for me to read. Aloud, I read the text:

"Death's door resides in the waters of sirens; one must venture to the Nagas' sacred island;

And in those waters lies the treasure of old; A lunar legacy forged of gold;

A champion of two souls made to seal the eclipse of its wrongdoing; shall bring a new hope through honest fate and challenged pursuing."

"You can understand it, Mala? Wow! For years, I have always wanted to know what this text said, and you figured it out! Destiny led you to find it!" yelled *Lolo Alma*. I feel his aura spike in excitement. *Lolo Alma* laughs, astonished, like I have cracked a code to a puzzle. Then, I see his face change to confusion, "But tell me, *Anak*, how could you read it?"

I want to tell him how I understand the script, but I hadn't realized that I could read *Baybayin* until this moment. "I'm not sure, *Lolo*," I say truthfully, "but this writing…I can't explain it, but it feels familiar like I have always known how to read it. I know it doesn't make sense, but I felt this strong power flow within me when I touched the copper-plate inscription."

This is it—Lolo Alma is going to think I am a monster, too—just like the other citizens of Zambo.

Lolo Alma takes a brief moment. He closes his eyes and rubs his chin, deep in thought. "This is a significant find! Looks like you won't need to find someone to translate it after all. You have a special gift. First the vision of dreams and now this talk of power. It's amazing! I remember the way Lau used to talk about it, too, how it felt like a flow of energy, but I wish I knew more, *Anak*. Maybe you have connections to the spirit world, too, just like my dear friend," he says.

I feel a strong sense of relief and surprise to see *Lolo Alma* so receptive. He celebrated my difference. *He even called it a gift.*

But what does this mean? Maybe Lolo Alma is onto something. Connections to the spirit world! I know I can read the inscription, but I still can't decipher the meaning. *I need to find another Babaylan for sure that can help me solve this mystery.*

Lolo Alma points at the hourglass by his bed frame, "It's getting late, *Anak*. The sun is setting. I think it's time for you to go home. But what an auspicious discovery."

"*Salamat, Lolo*, for showing me this copperplate. Is it really okay if I take with me?"

"It was never mine to keep, *Anak*. I believe it's your time now to carry this message and find a way to decipher its meaning. Go find your purpose for my old dear friend, Lau, who couldn't finish theirs."

I nod and understand, "*Maraming Salamat,*[11] again, *Lolo Alma*. I have to go tell my *Kuya* about this." Without delay, I put the copperplate in my pouch bag and sling it over my shoulder. I give *Lolo Alma* a big hug before scurrying out the secret chamber doors leaving the *Aklatan* in its magnificent wake.

---

11   Maraming Salamat - Thank you very much

CHAPTER 2

A VISIT FROM DEATH

Mala

I make my way exiting the outskirts of *Zambo*, the sun beginning to set behind me. The liveliness of the market that projected loud dwindled down to empty streets; The silent ambient sound of the incoming of night is the only aura leftover. I start to run, excited about the news. I can't wait to tell Salem about what I have discovered.

Light still passes dimly through the sky, painted in a reddish-orange hue. I make my way back home through the forest trail, the copperplate's message still in the back of my mind. I can't shake the feeling of the energy resonating within my body, how the excitement of it makes me feel less alone in this world. *Shamans exist! One of them must have the answer to the meaning of my dreams.*

But as I continue my stroll in the woods, my familiar walk home starts to feel somewhat exposed. I sense a different and strong energy that was not harmonious with the songs of the forest. Behind me, I can feel a new hymn. It is cold. A new melody hums its tune until suddenly a swarm of black moths fly swiftly past my face.

My body feels heavy, and I take a deep breath. As I turn around, I see the swarm of moths circulate over top each other. At first, they just fly around, but then they form into a shape that looks like a black hole.

And then a voice begins to echo as the swarm of moths melts away into the darkness of the shape, "How rude of you, taking this long to find it!"

The dark shape is a portal and out steps a large man. He is tall and muscular with umber brown skin, his melanin glowing in the sun's setting light. He has white tattoos that line around his arms, chest, and face. His eyes glow a deep golden hue, matching the light that bathes the forest. His hair is not hair at all, but a smoky black dust wisping in the air. He wears a golden crown with two large horns and his waist is draped in a beautiful, red silk tapestry touching the ground. His presence is immense, and the air suddenly becomes cold. I have never felt this kind of presence before.

"What are you?" I say shakily.

"Don't you mean who am I? Why don't you know? I am the Prince of Oblivion, the Keeper of Souls, the last whisper before a final breath." The divine man approaches me, their face closes in on mine. "I am *Sidapa*[12]—the Deity of Death."

I feel my chest tighten. It is harder to breathe. *Death. This is it. My fate ends here before it even begins.* I can't control my body shaking—my response to this pressure and fear. The sudden cold air doesn't help either.

"Is it...," I gulp, "my time, oh Deity of Death?"

Sidapa gives me a startled look. He starts to laugh, his expressions of amusement pervading through the entire forest.

---

12   Sidapa – Deity of Death; King of Underworld

"I am much more than the bringer of bad news. I am here because you are the new keeper of the copperplate, and I am here to verify if you are, in fact, the *right one*. And you can call me *Sidapa*. I may be a god, but I respect the work of *Babaylans*. You are a *Babaylan*, are you not?" he asks.

"I'm sorry, I think you have me mistaken for someone else. I am no *Babaylan*. I'm just a child from *Zambo*."

"Well, I'm not too sure about that," he says, crossing his massive arms. "I felt the energy of the copperplate revive just a few moments ago. Only a person with strong spiritual ties to our realm can activate magic like that."

He must be talking about when I first stumbled upon the copperplate in the Aklatan.

"Interesting," *Sidapa* says as he rubs his chin, "This is all very different. Even if you are not a trained shaman, you have some powerful magic in you," he confirms. "Regardless of the fact, it has awakened in you now! The question is are you the *right* keeper of the plate?"

"The right keeper?" I ask.

"Yes, you see, the last *Babaylan* who had the copperplate artifact was a very talented and powerful shaman. But she was not the one. She lacked a particular element that is required for the plate to awaken."

"I'm not sure what that element is, myself. But I don't think I have it," I say with discomfort in my voice.

Sidapa raises a brow to challenge me, "I think you doubt yourself too much," he says. He is right, I have a bad habit of doubting what I can do. I am not like Salem, a hunter and soon-to-be hero-warrior of *Zambo*. But I can't ignore this innate ability inside of me, either. Not anymore. I must recognize how I can always feel the energy of people, animals, trees, and the Earth. It means something more.

"Forgive me for not explaining it sooner. Shall we get more comfortable?" and with a snap of his fingers, the swarm of moths fly behind the two of us to form a pair of chairs. The chair looks to be made of a stainless obsidian black stone. The shape of the backrest of the chair is designed like a butterfly or moth.

"Please, sit," he gestures, and I take a seat as instructed. "Now, for centuries, I have been the guardian of the copperplate, the inscription you found is a prophecy to be completed by the champion, the rightful owner of the artifact."

I lean in, intrigued by the words flowing out of *Sidapa's* mouth. *A prophecy to be completed. Could I be the one?*

"The copperplate is the key to finding the Mask of Gold," *Sidapa* continues.

This is it! This artifact is the answer to my dream, to finding the mask!

"But as I've mentioned, the key can only be activated by the hands of the *right Babaylan*—the shaman to carry the lunar legacy of the prophecy."

"Lunar legacy?"

"Yes, the *Babaylan* who draws significant power from the Moon itself. There is only one who can," he notes.

"That makes sense. I think the copperplate inscription said something about that, but I wasn't sure what it meant."

"Oh! So, you can read *Baybayin*. Impressive, but expected for many practicing *Babaylans* of this time. Most days, the knowledge of the *Baybayin* script has been lost and only a few communities still use it across the islands. If you're not a *Babaylan*, then how could you read it? It is not taught to these kinds of lands—those lands overtaken by the Blood Moon Knights," *Sidapa* says with a painful expression.

"Well, when I first saw the copperplate, I felt this wave of energy flow inside of me. The same one that must have summoned you here. One moment it was all just symbols, and then the next thing I knew I could make meaning out of the message. Like these symbols were familiar, and that I've read them before. And before finding the plate, I had a dream! Some sort of vision that led me to finding the artifact."

"A dream, you say?" he inquires, "And you're sure you're not a *Babaylan*? The shamans could see elaborate and spectacular visions in their dreams. Divination they call it."

"Well I'm not sure about anything anymore," I say with a deep breath. "That was exactly why I was looking for this inscription in the first place. I was hoping to find clues to discover the meaning of my dreams. I still can't make sense of it —waking up in a garden of purple flowers. I've never been in that garden before."

Alerted, *Sidapa* asks, "Purple flowers? These flowers were in your dream? Could you describe them?" I had the full attention of the Deity of Death.

"Yes. In the dream there were these beautiful flowers that smelled of vanilla and glowed like stars. It was as if these purple flowers were lined with a white cast. They reminded me of the moonlight, but now that I think of it, I didn't see the Moon in the sky. Only stars."

"Interesting, very interesting indeed," *Sidapa* takes a moment to think. "I believe what you described to me are the *Takay Flowers*.[13] These are flowers of the Moon created by my one and only love, *Bulan*.[14]"

---

13 *Takay Flowers* – Purple water hyacinth; gift from the lunar deity; legend is native to the Bicolano people

14 Bulan – One of the Seven Moon Deities; The Last Moon

"*Bulan?*" I ask. *That must've been the voice that called out to me in my dreams. Did my spirit arrive to Bulan's domain? and how?* "Are they another Deity like you?"

"A deity like me? I can only fathom. I remember it like it was yesterday. The first moment I saw *Bulan* was when he and his Moon siblings first visited this Earth. The seven of them, silver light in body, but eyes each of a different color—reflecting those of the rainbow. They bathed in the Enchanted Lake of the island of sirens—the *Isla Sirena*. The *Nagas* and I felt as if we were pulled by their gravity and were brought out of our dark underground to witness their lunar grace from the heavens."

"*Nagas?*" I ask.[15]

"Mermaid serpents that help guard the gates of the Underworld. Water spirits that protect the secrets of the dead," he clarifies and continues, "And just like that, I saw *Bulan*, the way his silver hair drifted in the wind. I stared at his amethyst eyes as he played and swam with the fishes of the lake; his tenderness evoked such tranquility across the waters that even the fish danced with him to witness his elegance. It was love at first sight. His beauty and his grace could even bring life to death!"

I listened to the beauty of *Sidapa*'s words, and it made my heart warm to hear his love story.

"But alas, my time with my silver lover grew short," his expressions of euphoria transform to a tone of sorrow, "*Bakunawa*, you see, was a *Naga*, too, before."

"*Bakunawa*...as in the Deity of Eclipses?" I ask, shocked.

He nods, "Yes, before she was a deity, her true, original form was a mermaid serpent. She was not just any *Naga*; she

---

15 Nagas – Water spirits; sea serpent deities that guard the gates of the Underworld; Keepers of treasure, wealth, and secrets of the dead

was the most powerful guardian of the dark depths of these waters. She too, like the rest of us Underworldly spirits, fell in love with one of the Moon siblings that bathed in our Earth's water. *Bulan's* sister, *Haliya*."

"What happened?" I ask.

"Her heart was broken by *Haliya*—an unrequited love.[16] She let the pain and anger of her heartbreak consume her. She hid, at first, in the depths of the Enchanted Lake's darkness until the pain grew to be too much, and she caused a great earthquake that had rumbled the core of the islands. Consumed by her madness, she transformed into a serpent-like dragon, and from the depths of the waters, she flew above to great heights to enact her revenge. She devoured the Moon siblings one by one, leaving *Bulan* to be the last Moon. This is when she became known as the Deity of Eclipses, and why a lunar eclipse is known as the Blood Moon today."

"Representing the blood of the Moon siblings devoured," I say.

"Precisely," he agrees with a grave expression, "*Bakunawa*, The Moon Eater."

I begin to feel my anxiety grow stronger. *We're dealing with The Moon Eater. How can I go up against that? I'm only a child!* My body begins to shake once again.

Before I have time to notice, the sun finally finishes setting and the darkness of night fills the sky. I feel the wave of energy again as I stare at the Moon's light. *Was Bulan watching us from up there?* The Moon graced us with its beauty, shining its lunar light in the forest. My fears began to leave my body. Calm. Yes, just like *Sidapa* had mentioned about *Bulan*, the Moon's presence helped to calm my nerves. *But*

---

16   Haliya – One of the Seven Moon Deities; The Golden Moon

how can I still see in the darkness of the forest? I think to myself, *The Moon is bright, but never bright enough to light up the night like this.*

"Ah, now I see," *Sidapa* smiles, "Oh, things have played out very interestingly! You are the true owner of the copperplate!" He shouts, reaching his hands outwards toward me, "Take a look at for yourself."

I look down and see that my hands are glowing brightly. My tan brown skin flashes a white and silver luminescence, and I see my body surrounded by a bright white light.

"I—I'm glowing!" I yell. My body has never channeled energy like this before. It feels different than simply noticing the energy around me. This time, it feels like a river, flowing inside of me like a waterfall and pouring outward. It is as if I am back there, in my dream, in the garden of *Takay Flowers. Yes, like I am a Takay Flower glowing with the stars in the beautiful night sky.*

I want to feel beautiful like those flowers, but then I start to realize how scary all of this is. *The people of Zambo will hate me even more, now. To them, I am already like a monster, but to be shining like this, the Blood Moon Knights will surely treat me the way they did Lau, the last Babaylan of Zambo.* I start to feel anxious, and then I feel the river flowing inside me disrupt. The light of my glow slowly begins to fade and dissipate away, bringing darkness back into night.

"The branch by you—grab that for me, will you, my dear?" I grab the branch and, with a snap of his fingers, *Sidapa* lights a fire on the branch, creating light for us in the night. "Yes, it looks to me that you carry the element for which I've been searching. I've been looking for years, but you have yet to fully control it," *Sidapa* confirms, "The lunar legacy—you are the one chosen by the Moon. It is your duty to bring that copperplate to the last Moon, *Bulan*. There, you will find the Mask of Gold and end the tyranny of the Blood Moon Knights once and for all."

"But, how could this be? End the tyranny of the knights? What do you mean?" I cannot help but think of Salem in this moment. He is going to be initiated into the Blood Moon Knights with a ritual tomorrow.

"Like I said, the copperplate is the key. It must have activated your inner spiritual connection with the Moon. I am very aware of the Blood Moon Knights and their deadly agenda. I know they are violent," *Sidapa* barks.

"Sadly, the last *Babaylan* who owned the copperplate died years ago at their hands," I say, thinking of *Lolo Alma*.

"I assure you, the past owner of the copperplate is resting peacefully now," *Sidapa* replies.

I smile, "That's good to hear. I hope to tell my *Lolo Alma* that sometime. I'm sure he'll be happy to know she is at peace."

"But our current world is not at peace. As the prophecy foretells, you must find the Mask of Gold before the *Bakunawa* is able to locate it. She is also searching for the Mask of Gold and plans to find it before the next Lunar eclipse. This will occur four nights after tonight."

"To finish what she couldn't years ago," I say, amazed.

"Yes, and the Blood Moon Knights will be aiding her in finding and destroying it. The bearer of the Mask of Gold almost defeated *Bakunawa* in the Great Battle of Moons."

"The Great Battle of Moons?"

"*Haliya* forged the Mask of Gold from the tears that flowed from her amber eyes. These tears gave her the strength to avenge her fallen siblings. Like a warrior from the sky, she graced this Earth once again and challenged the *Bakunawa* in the Great Battle to try and defeat her."

"I'm guessing she didn't win," I say.

"The battle might have been lost, but the true fight is still not over. The *Bakunawa* is at her most vulnerable and has grown weak from the Great Battle. This is why she is in hiding and has enlisted the aid of the Blood Moon Knights. Because of *Haliya's* sacrifice, *Bulan* has been protected."

"This is all too much to handle. How can I end this? You're a god. Can't you deliver this message to him yourself?"

"Alas, only the champion of the prophecy is powerful enough to defeat the Deity of Eclipses, the one to find the Mask of Gold and finish the Great Battle of Moons. Ever since then, my lover has hidden himself away on the Moon far from my reach here on Earth, away from the clutches of *Bakunawa*. Through the power of spiritual faith, the people of the islands have protected *Bulan* from *Bakunawa* with their strong beliefs and rituals. These provide energy to *Bulan*—enough strength to protect himself from each lunar eclipse. But as the Blood Moon Knights' empire grows stronger, so does the power of the Deity of Eclipses. And with every passing lunar eclipse, *Bakunawa* grows stronger. Eventually she will be able to break through the Moon's protection. And on the next Lunar Eclipse, she will once again turn into the Great Serpent Dragon that flies to reach the Moon and enact her final revenge onto my love, *Bulan*, in his most vulnerable state."

I take another deep breath and a moment passes as I try to process what this all means. I look up at *Sidapa* to find him staring at me, his cosmic energy demanding an answer. *Am I up for the task?*

"So, it's a race. A race to find the Mask of Gold," I say.

Sidapa nods, "Find *Bulan*, procure the mask, and end the Great Battle of Moons that never finished. Protect the people of the islands from the demise of the upcoming Blood Moon.

The prophecy has chosen you to complete it. You must venture to the place where it all began, the *Isla Sirena*. I must warn you; the *Isla Sirena* is an island of strong magical presence. It is dangerous to anyone courageous enough to venture there. Because of the nature of the island, the spirits and beasts residing there can be seen by mortals. Once you have reached the island, you must meet the *Nagas* that reside in the Enchanted Lake. They will help to you to fulfill your quest."

I could not help but doubt myself as the right choice of this journey. "Why me?" I ask. "Why now? I wish I were strong enough, like my brother, to fight and protect this world!"

"Being you is a gift, is it not?" *Sidapa* says, "Wishes come true for those destined, those who are brave enough to chase them."

I nod and understand. I have always wished for better for myself, but now I have the opportunity to act. Being different starts to feel like a gift— one the Moon has bestowed upon me. *How can I say no to this call? In just a day, my entire life has changed.* I finally feel that I have a purpose, a mission.

"I will find my way to *Isla Sirena*."

Sidapa stands up from his seat. He smiles and claps his hands, sending a wave of energy and gust throughout the entire forest. "Great!" he yells, "That's what I like to hear. You'll need to follow the *Takay Flower* Constellation," *Sidapa* points to the night sky, and I see a starry constellation shaped like the flowers in my dream. Seven petals line the night sky. The stars sparkle vivaciously, with one of the stars burning brighter than the others. "That brightest star on the top of the north petal is known as the North Star. That is the Goddess *Tala's*[17] anchor to the sky. She put it there so she would never

---

17   Tala – Deity of Stars

be lost as she dances from star to star throughout the galaxy. When you follow the North Star you will always know where you are headed and will eventually find the *Isla Sirena*."

I realize I need Salem, someone who can sail a boat on the waters off the shore while I navigate and follow the North star. "I need to go and see my *Kuya*," I say, "I can't do this quest without him."

Sidapa waves his hands and dissipates the obsidian chairs, turning them back into moths. "Many lives depend on you," *Sidapa* reminds me.

He does a final nod as a gesture of goodwill and enters back into his portal. Before he fully vanishes back to his Underworld realm, he echoes, "And when you see my love, tell him I'm *dying* to see him again." The black energy transforms back into a swarm of moths that disperse and fly away into the forages of the trees and bushes, leaving a trail of smoke behind.

I can do this, I think to myself. My confidence strengthens. And I actually believe I can.

CHAPTER 3

AN ULTIMATUM

___

Salem

At the Temple of Serpents, the Blood Moon Knights and I close out our final training for the pre-ceremony preparations before the initiation. I sit back and finally relax after another long day. As I lie down, I look around me and gaze at the marble obelisks— scores of obelisks stand along the temple grounds. I look over the passing view of the City of *Zambo*, where the temple hinges on top of the tallest hill overlooking the grand view of the city.

"Great work today, men! You will all be fine warriors. The *Bakunawa*, our Great Serpent Goddess, would be pleased to see you all herself if she could," shouts the Knight Leader Baskel who pats a heavy hand on my back, the force pushing me slightly forward, "Especially you, hunter boy. You proved us well, and we expect great things from you."

"Thank you, Sir Baskel," I say, stretching my arms. I know I must build as much stamina as I can to endure the final step to be recognized as a Blood Moon Knight.

The final ceremony is known as the Blood Moon Pact. It is an ancient, secret blood ritual that ties us warriors together as brothers-in-arms. I will recite the oath to swear my loyalty to the *Bakunawa* and the warriors with the others. While reciting our oath, we will cut our palms, each from the sacred Serpent's Dagger. I haven't seen the dagger myself yet, but we will all witness its glory on the night of the ritual. Our blood will be drawn and mixed together as we offer it to the *Bakunawa*. The ceremony will complete the initiation, and I will finally become a recognized Blood Moon Knight just like Baskel.

Temple keepers dressed in blood red robes left their stone building, baskets of meat and fish in their hands.

"These are gifts from the Temple of Serpents for the work and dedication to the Great *Bakunawa*, please take them home to you and your families and celebrate," says Baskel.

One of the temple keepers approaches me. Her face is partially hidden by the robe hood, but I can tell that she is beautiful. She smiles and hands me the food.

"*Salamat*," I say blushing at her.

She nods silently and smiles back. Then she turns back to join the rest of the temple keepers as they return inside. I notice she looks back and waves. I feel my cheeks warm further and wave back.

The sun begins to set, and I need to be home to prepare dinner. As I pack up the last of my belongings and make my way home, the soldiers-in-training groups together and begins to march downtown to the city tavern. One of them notices that I am headed home and stops me.

"Salem!" One of the men yells, "Come join us for drinks to celebrate before the initiation!"

"You guys have fun without me. I have to be home to take care of dinner for my brother. I can't let these gifts of food go to waste."

"You mean your sister?" one of the other men yells back. His long black hair is tied into a ponytail, the end hitting the sweat on his brown neck. His voice reminds me of an annoying crow. Tagyo, the most arrogant and obnoxious warrior in our group, looks me in the eyes and I sense his hubristic personality, stemming from ego. "The monster of *Zambo*," he mocks.

I clench my fists. I feel my body heat up, my anger boiling at the remark. Without a second thought, I take a step toward the men, ready to fight the warrior for daring to mock my brother. Tagyo is as tall as I am, and a great warrior. *But I can take him. If he wants to challenge my family, he can deal with me.*

Before I even get the chance to draw my sword, Baskel appears and places his arm in front of me, stopping me in my tracks. "That's enough, men!" he commands.

"Yes, sir!" the warriors all say. I glare at Tagyo as he heads out to leave with the rest of the men.

"Don't mind them. They will be your brothers-in-arms soon and will learn to respect you. Head home, Salem. We will see you tomorrow for the ceremony," Baskel says. I nod silently, but I am still upset by the incident. Baskel gives me another pat on the back and starts to walk back toward the city while I head home.

While walking back, I cannot not help but continue to feel frustrated that I can't adequately defend Mala. I am always overprotective over my little brother. *How can I respect men who can't respect me and my family? The people of Zambo, the citizens and the warriors, all respect me as a hunter and now knight-to-be. But when it comes to my brother, the people can never accept them. Sometimes I am just as confused as the citizens.* Mala's feminine expression scares those who haven't grown up with us. But it's just how Mala is, that doesn't make them deserving of hate. Even though I have never fully understood Mala's journey with their identity, I have always loved them unconditionally and will never let such insults slide.

Finally, I reach home. I try not to carry my anger from the incident into our home, but I can still taste my rage in my mouth. Back in the kitchen, I begin preparing dinner, cooking up the rice, fish and meat that was gifted by the Temple Keepers. *I could get used to these prizes and the glory of being a warrior.*

As I finish preparing dinner, I cannot help but think of how I have been training for this moment for most of my life. To finally be respected and have a place of power in the city, maybe this will lead Father to finally recognize me and bring his attention to his own children. *No, in fact, I will be better than Father. What kind of warrior is he? One with no honor for his family.*

As I finish preparing the meal, I notice the night falling and begin to wonder about Mala's whereabouts. It is getting late, and Mala usually comes home before I do.

Just when I decide to go out looking for them, my *Ading* rushes into the house slamming the door open behind them.[18] They look shaken up.

"Little brother, what's wrong? Are you okay?" I ask, concerned.

---

18   Ading – Younger sibling

"I'm—I'm fine," Mala stutters as they catch their breath. "I ran home—I had a day you won't believe."

Before they can continue, I grab a bowl and a large wooden spoon. I scoop rice into a bowl and add the cooked meat and fish on top, watching the steam rise off the meal, and hand it over to them.

"*Kuya*, I—"

I put a finger over my own mouth to quiet them mid-sentence. "First, eat."

Mala takes a deep breath and, with their hands, scoops the rice with some of the meat into their mouth. They chew ferociously, trying to finish the bowl.

"Slow down, will you? I know my cooking is good, but you have to let it settle slowly as you eat," I gloat.

Mala slams the empty bowl of food on the table. I stare at the bowl, impressed.

"I was starving," Mala explains.

"You're telling me," I respond, "I've never seen you eat this fast before. So, what is this dire news you are dying to tell me about?"

"Dying to tell you..." Mala chuckles, "Well, it definitely involves Death."

"Ha ha," I laugh sarcastically, "Now what's this about? Are you okay?"

"I don't know, *Kuya*," they say. They shift anxiously in their chair.

"You know you can tell me anything. You're my little brother; I have your back no matter what," I try to reassure them.

Mala lifts their head up and takes another deep breath. "I'm leaving *Zambo*, Salem, and I need you to come with me," they say with a straight face, their eyes wide open.

At first, I can't believe my ears, and I laugh. "Time to stop being funny, Mala. Leaving? What do you mean 'leave?'" I start to say in a more serious tone. I don't understand why Mala wants to leave the life and home I built for both of us here, in *Zambo*.

"I know you have a lot on your mind lately. With the initiation tomorrow for the Blood Moon Knights and everything, but *Kuya,* you have to listen to me. You can't go. You can't do this."

"I can't go?" I challenge them, my rage from earlier burning once again in my stomach. "You don't call the shots here, little brother. I've been working hard for this for a long time. I'm doing all this for us since Father won't!"

How can my own brother say that? I feel betrayed—like all the work I have done to provide for us was for nothing.

Mala continues to speak frantically, "You need to listen to me. I had a dream this morning. About a woman and a Mask of Gold. And then the Keeper of the *Aklatan, Lolo Alma,* showed me a secret chamber where I found a copperplate inscription which turned out to be an ancient prophecy that summoned *Sidapa,* the Deity of Death. I—I met Death, and I started glowing! Like, really glowing in the middle of our conversation and he—"

"I don't want to hear it!" I interrupt as I get up from my seat. *Talk of dreams and meeting deities?* I think, *Mala is lying.* I slam my hands on the table, shaking the floor. "We're not going anywhere. End of conversation. You need to stop talking about this now."

Mala flinches slightly but manages to get up from their seat. "You aren't listening to me, *Kuya.* Lives are at stake. You can't just tell me what to do just because you are going to be a warrior soon. The Blood Moon Knights are going to hurt people if we don't stop them!"

"They've only ever protected the citizens of *Zambo!*" I yell. "Who do you think is the reason we even had a meal to eat tonight? Think with your head, little brother. We need them to survive and to have a better life."

"There won't be a life to live if we don't do anything to stop them before the next lunar eclipse."

In my frustrated state, I take a moment to recollect my thoughts. "Eclipse? What about the next lunar eclipse?"

"Don't you see, *Kuya?* When they initiate you tomorrow, you won't be protecting anyone. In the next few days—on the lunar eclipse—you will be under the full control of *Bakunawa.* I can't sit by and watch you become controlled by her."

"Mala, what is this all about? You're not making any sense."

Then Mala grabs a shiny item out of their bag. It looks like a copperplate, but I cannot understand the inscription written over it.

"Like I said, after my dream—about the woman with the Mask of Gold—I went to the *Aklatan* to find answers. *Lolo Alma* showed me this copperplate. It is the only relic that the Blood Moon Knights weren't able to destroy. The inscription tells of a prophecy of the one with the lunar legacy to find the Mask of Gold. The knights killed the old generation who fought back against them when they first invaded here, Salem. They aren't here to protect us!"

It is all too much. I sit down again, just process it all. *This whole time the warrior way was a lie?* I can't fathom it. The glory, the way the citizens praised us; the training and the warriors I grew fond of in my time here at *Zambo*, are all a lie.

"You're lying," I assert. I can't take hearing any more of Mala's dreams and fantasy stories. "You just want to leave because no one likes you here. Why can't you be normal for once?" I scream out of anger. But the moment the words leave my mouth, I regret them.

Mala winces.

"I'm sorry Mala, I didn't mean that," I try to apologize, but I know the damage has been done. *But how can I trust them? None of it makes sense: gods, spirits, and now some made up prophecy from a copperplate with unknown writing.*

Mala sighs deeply and gives me a displeased look, "It's not about me not having friends, *Kuya*. It's true, I never felt like I belonged to this city and its people. I could never make the bonds with the citizens the way you have with the community and the warriors. I have always felt different, but that never stopped me from loving and caring about them—about life. But now I have found out I have a gift, something that was innate within me this whole time," they pause, looking at their hands. "I have to leave and find that mask."

I shut my eyes and pretend not to listen to them. Although I can hear every word, I don't want to listen. I know what Mala is saying was something they believe, and the guilt of this knowledge weighs on me. *They really plan to leave our home.*

"*Kuya*, I need you," they beg, "I can't do this myself—let alone sail a boat to another island!"

Still silent, I choose not to answer.

"Fine. I am going with or without you," they say. Mala puts the copperplate back in their bag and starts walking out the door.

I sit in silence. I just need some space to think clearly. A few moments pass and I begin to recall the details that would take place on the night of the final ritual. It calls for a sacrifice of my life. I know it will be a heavy sacrifice; I will no longer have to hunt for food day and night to feed us. But I do enjoy hunting—it feels like a part of my identity. I am a provider, and the rush of the hunt excites me to my core. Mala's warning, though, keeps ringing in my head. *A warrior worthy of protecting and serving the city of Zambo.* That resolve is what made me want to become a knight in the first place.

But protect them from what, exactly? I ask myself. *No, I'm going to be a Blood Moon Knight,* I tell myself. I never dare to question the Blood Moon Knights and their objectives. The ritual has always been a secret tradition. I will eventually discover the reasons to serve once I am finally initiated. My goal is to get in, become stronger than I am now, and prove my honor to the city. I can't afford to quit, not this close to the goal.

After all, I am to become a warrior not for the sake of the Great Serpent, but to provide for my family. *My family. Yes, Mala is my only family left. Mother is dead; Father abandoned us—he chose the life of a warrior over his life with his children. Wouldn't I just be following in his footsteps? What would it all be for if I don't have my little brother anymore?*

I have my answer.

On the outskirts of the city of *Zambo* lies the main port at the end of the peninsula. I can see the handful of unmanned fishing boats resting on the beach. The villagers rely on these fishing boats to trade; I fish these waters from time to time with the rest of the fishermen.

While walking on the beach, the soles of my feet touch the white sand; it is powdery and silky, soft, yet firm. The night is quiet except for the tides of the shore's waves crashing lightly under the clear night sky. Amongst those fishing vessels resides the *vintas*.[19] The *vinta*s are characterized by their colorful shapes that are stitched on the sails, a rainbow of vibrant printed patterns. The prows and sterns resemble the gaping mouth of a crocodile, a symbol of the protector of the island. Walking the beaches of the port, I see Mala from afar. They are near the shores. They are trying to push a *vinta* off the beach, their efforts unsuccessful. I rush to assist them. Their long black hair is frazzled from the gust of the ocean air. Their light blue skirt robe digs deep into the sand as they try to push the heavy weight of the boat.

As I get closer, I see the *vinta*, its magnificent structure sitting on the sands of the beach close to the bedrocks of the waves. Most *vinta*s are smaller—about five meters long—but the one Mala chose is larger than usual. It is tied down from the shaft to one of the bedrocks near the sea to prevent the water from moving it away from the shore. Mala must not have seen it. I quickly glide across the sand onto the rope to untie it from its haul.

"So, we're stealing ships now?" I joke as I start to untie some ropes that are anchoring the wooden boat.

"Stealing? No, just borrowing it for the days until the Lunar Eclipse is over—I fully intend to give it back," they say, continuing to push the *vinta*. After untying the rope, I join them and the two of us begin to push the boat together onto the shallow waters.

"You're not here to stop me are you, *Kuya*?" Mala says with a touch of hostility in their voice.

---

19   Vinta – Traditional outrigger board made by the local Zamboanga City people living in the archipelago; based on Philippine island of Mindanao

I roll my eyes and say, "One, two, push!" ignoring my brother's question. The *vinta* is heavy, but together, we manage to slide the boat across the sands.

"One, two, push!" I shout again.

With the two of us pushing, our toes digging deep into the sand, we move the *vinta* slowly into the shallow waters. The cool waves crash onto our feet and legs.

"One, two push!" Mala shouts, joining in.

The boat finally floats into the water. I grab Mala and push them up onto the inside of the boat. I quickly jump over the edge and hop inside as well. The *vinta* is spacious, allowing enough room for both of us to lie within the ship. This is a simple ship with a sail and paddle. *As long as the seas are gentle, I can ensure a safe passage to our destination—wherever that is.*

"Are you sure you want to come? It's going to be dangerous. It's not too late to swim back to shore," says Mala.

I roughly rub them on the head, "What kind of older brother would I be to let you go on a dangerous adventure alone?"

"*Salamat, Kuya.*"

I nod and put my hands on my thighs, looking over to Mala, "I really am sorry, little brother. I didn't mean what I said earlier about wanting you to be normal."

Mala lightly punches me on the shoulder. "Ow!" I yell, pretending it hurt more than it actually did.

"All is forgiven. One day you will see. My difference is a gift. Normal was never the life I should have accepted to live anyway," they say as they touch the waters of the ocean with their hands.

I can't help but smile. I am happy to hear this from Mala, knowing how difficult it must have felt to be treated poorly by the citizens of *Zambo. But we'll show them. We'll prove them wrong. As long as I can be there to protect them and help them on their journey — that's what the true warrior way is, anyways.* I look up at the sky and ask, "So, where are we going exactly, and do you know how to get there?"

Mala smiles back. "We must follow the *Takay Flower* Constellation, the North Star on the top petal will be our map," they point up to the sky.

Yes, I can see it—the beautiful flower-shaped constellation, "Wow," I whisper to myself.

"To the *Isla Sirena*," Mala smiles.

CHAPTER 4

THE *VINTA*

Salem

On the *vinta*, Mala and I sit together; the night is still young, as the waxing Moon shines bright. Within the *vinta* are a few supplies: a knife, a fishing net, a blanket, a brass oil lamp with little oil left, a long bamboo stick, and a pair of large wooden paddles. I brought my sword from my trainings with the Blood Moon Knights and my *pana*,[20] and a bundle of arrows carried in a long, narrow quiver made of stitched cloth that I use for hunting.

I grab the lamp and turn it on slowly, a small spark of fire shining brightly. Mala holds the blanket in their arms and walks over to me. They wrap the blanket around our shoulders, and the two of us huddle closely in front of the lamp in an attempt to stay warm.

"Mala," I whisper as they turn their head to face me. "I need to know if you're okay."

Mala is quiet at first, looking unsure of what to say. *They must have a lot on their mind.*

---

20 Pana – Traditional wooden bow

"I'm not sure," they reply. They look up at the sky, their brown eyes glimmering in the moonlight. They lift their right arm and point at the Moon. "All I know is that I was chosen by the Moon."

"Chosen by the Moon?" I inquire again, this time really wanting to understand what Mala was saying.

Mala proceeds to explain the events that happened before our fight at the house. This time around, I listen to it all—no arguments or interruptions. I try to absorb as much of what happened to them during that day—how their dream led them to the *Aklatan* where Keeper Alma showed them the copperplate, how they felt a wave of energy within them that let them read in *Baybayin*, how *Sidapa*, the God of Death, was summoned to tell them about the prophecy, and how we ended up here, sailing on a *vinta* to visit a magical island that may or may not be real. *All this to find a Mask of Gold that also may or may not be real.*

The part of it all that strikes me the most is, all this time, Mala has had an ability to feel the energies of people, animals, trees, and the Earth.

"If you can really feel energies, what do mine feel like?" I ask.

Mala takes a moment to think. They stare deeply at the lamp, gazing at the fire's blaze. Then, they giggle.

Maybe I give off bad vibes?

"Warm, like a fire. But not too hot like a heat that is meant to burn. No, the energy you give off is more of a cozy kind of warmth like a blazing stone-lined hearth. The vibrations that I grew up to know and trust. I can feel the desire of your fire. It wants to grow as bright as the rays of the sun."

"Wow, really?" I ask.

"You'll get there *Kuya*, I feel it. You never let that fire burn out. But it does get scary sometimes when you get upset or angry. But that's okay because that's just who you are."

"Yeah, I'm working on my temper," I acknowledge. *It hasn't been easy, but I'm happy to know Mala accepts me too for who I am. I need to do the same.* "So, how about the part about you glowing? Why aren't you glowing right now?"

"I can't seem to control it. I know the copperplate awakened my powers, but I'm not sure what triggers my connection with the Moon—that's why we need to find a *Babaylan* when we reach the island."

I nod slowly. I may not see it, but I trust Mala's words and judgement. They have always been special.

"Have you always known this power, Mala? To feel the energies around you?"

"Remember the time Father came home from his trip to the northern islands right after he was initiated as a Blood Moon Knight? I was probably nine years old."

"Yes, I remember. You held onto me and asked me not to leave your side."

"I remember it vividly; I could *feel* Father's energy. It was like something had changed during his trip. Like, he did something that changed his entire demeanor. It was the first time I could feel he wasn't the same person anymore, like his soul was…stained."

"Yeah…," I say. "I remember the day, too. That's when he started becoming distant. Never home to take care of us. Always on duty for the Blood Moon Knights. That's when I started to learn how to hunt and fish just for us to get by."

"We were so young at the time; I don't think we recognized what had happened. But now looking back, I know.

What I felt was real. His spirit changed when he became a Blood Moon Knight. I could never articulate it before."

"Before that night, I remember he used to tell us stories of the Great *Bakunawa*," I said, "and how she would bring our city and people great fortune. How he would become a knight to honor Mother."

"Don't you see *Kuya*, it was all a lie."

Yes, Mala is right, I think. It all starts to make sense. A shadow had crept within *Zambo*, and slowly but surely, that shadow cast itself over the people, changing our beliefs and way of life.

I can't help but wonder why they never told me about these feelings of energy. "Why did you keep this from me, Mala?" I ask.

They tense up at the question. "Because *Kuya*, I was scared. Growing up, I was so different from you and the rest of the citizens of *Zambo*. I never fit in like you, Salem. I was treated like a monster for being too feminine. I didn't belong with any group except our family. I was all alone with this...curse. It only made me feel more isolated. I tried to suppress it for most of my life."

I am surprised to hear my little brother felt this way, but also I understand how I enabled it as well.

"Are you kidding me? This is so cool! The folks back at home are just jealous they can't be blessed like you," I say with a bright smile as I hug Mala. But what they said about being too feminine or masculine strikes me. I can't ignore it anymore. *How can I be so ignorant about their feelings?* "I'm sorry for not making it any better for you back at home. I always thought I did a good job in making our home feel more welcoming. I understand why you kept it a secret."

As Mala looked at me about to respond, I quickly say, "Before you say anything else, I want to say I'm sorry for our fight earlier. It's why you left to go on this quest alone. I thought I would never get the chance to apologize and say I'm sorry. I want you to know that I see you. All of you. I don't want to hurt you again the way that I did. I want to celebrate your difference, and it makes me proud to call you my sibling, my *Ading*. What do you prefer to be called?"

Mala's eyes widened. They take a long moment to pause and they smile. "*Kuya*, I will always be your *Ading*."

I smile back, "So, my *Ading*, are you a demi-deity now, too, or what?"

It seems that my words of reassurance helped to lessen Mala's anxiety and they began to relax, "No, *Kuya*, I'm not a demi-deity—at least I don't think I am. We have the same parents."

"Hmmm. Good point," I say as I place my hand on my chin to think of a counterpoint, "But why you, Mala? Why did the Moon choose you?"

"I don't know. I plan to ask *Bulan* when we find the Mask of Gold."

It looks like we have a long road ahead of us. But I'll be here to support them no matter what.

"Mala, you know what this means right?"

"What, Salem?"

I wrap my right arm around them and point to the water's empty abyss. With a huge grin I excitedly announce, "It means I'm hungry, and I need you to use your Moon magic to get us some fish! Whip up a huge wave onto the boat! We'll catch more than with our fishing net and bamboo, easily!"

Mala rolls their eyes and laughs off the joke. "That's not how it works, *Kuya*. I still don't know the full extent of this magic—I just know I can access it when I see the Moon. That's what *Sidapa* told me, as I am the lunar legacy." Mala gets up and peaks over the boat to touch the water. "But, you know, maybe that's how my Moon powers work. I used to read fairytales about the Moon, too, you know. In the *Aklatan*. Within the stories of fantasy and how the ocean has a spiritual relationship with the Moon." Mala gets up and places their hand over their heart, "and it's power over our spirit."

I look over at Mala with a concerned face.

Mala reacts by folding their arms and pouting, "You think I'm lying again!"

"No, no! I've just never read any of those stories and wouldn't know. But I see what you're saying. The tides of the sea are sometimes much stronger at night, as if being pulled by the Moon."

"Yes, like the Moon is the teacher of the waves. But it's just from stories. I can feel the energy of the waves right now. Under the *vinta*, the water here is tender and forbearing carrying a safe passage for us in the night," they look up at the sky.

"Maybe the Moon is looking out for us somehow with its relationship with the tides," I say.

"I'd like to believe so. I haven't talked to *Bulan*, so I wouldn't know," Mala says as they close their eyes, "So, why can't you go fishing right now?"

"I need more light. I don't want to risk losing the fish net or the spear."

"Right," Mala says. Then they look over to me, fear present in their eyes. "I'm scared, Salem."

I wrap my arm around Mala trying to comfort them. I tell them, "Don't worry, Mala, I'm scared too. But big brother's got you. Let's get some rest now"

And so we rest.

I feel the sun's rays scorching down my face. I wince and slowly open my eyes. The waters from last night were calm compared to the heavier rocking of the waves during the day. I inhale the pungent scent of saltwater in the air. My stomach begins to growl.

"You're awake now, *Kuya*," Mala says. As I get up from my sleep, I look up and see Mala standing over the edge of the *vinta*. "No dreams this time," they say.

With the morning sun's ray beaming brightly, the *Takay Flower* Constellation would not arrive until nightfall to lead us to our course. But now with light, I see some of the figures of smaller islands from afar. *This is good*, I think to myself. I can use these islands as a reference point to know our position during the day and not accidentally sail off course.

I grab the fishing net and cast it over the water. The rope of the net is tied to my left wrist, so I won't lose the net in the water. I grab the bamboo stick lying on the dock. I begin slapping the surrounding surface of the water. This is a unique fishing technique that is commonly practiced by the fishermen of *Zambo*. By slapping the water with the long bamboo, I scare the fish and other marine animals into our nets.

After a few moments pass, I start pulling up the fishing net. Steadily, I drag the net upward from the depths of the blue waters. When the full net comes to the surface, I see movement. *Perfect catch!* I think to myself as I pinch the top of the net to enclose and trap the fishes. I lift the net over the water and into the *vinta*. Excitedly, Mala comes over to see.

"Time for our morning meal," I look over to Mala with a grin.

"Finally, I'm starving," they say.

"Let's see what we got, *Ading*."

I shake out the net and slowly, a bunch of small fish fall out and flap around on the wooden boards of the boat. As I continue to shake, a larger fish plops out of the net. It has blue fins and yellow hues.

"Tuna!" I yell, proud of my victorious catch.

Mala observes as I start to prepare our meal for the day. I quickly grab the knife and fillet the side of the fish. The craft of my cuts are steadfast and unwavering as I slice the tuna into edible pieces. I take the first raw slice in my hand, inspecting it to make sure there were no bones and then give it to Mala.

"Here, take a bite," I offer.

Mala stares at it, first inspecting its deep red color—the blood of the fish still bleeding out of the meat.

"*Salamat, Kuya*," Mala says and then eats the slice.

I do the same. The tuna tastes savory with dense, firm texture. After eating the fish, I continue to sail the *vinta*, steering it with the paddle. I can't imagine Mala sailing these waters alone. They sat quietly, relaxing under the sun's heat, looking in deep contemplation. *They must be thinking about our next step for when we reach the island.*

As Mala begins to close their eyes, I decide to interrupt their relaxation. "Hey, *Ading!*" I yell at them. At first no response as Mala tries to ignore me and peacefully relax. "Remember when Father used to tell us stories about monsters when we were younger? How if we didn't go to bed early a *Manananggal*[21] would come at night to eat us?"

---

21 Manananggal – Malevolent, man-eating, and blood-sucking monster native to the Philippines.

"Yes, I do. Those stories used to give me nightmares," Mala finally responds.

Slowly, I turn my head to face Mala, "Well, it just had me thinking about something."

"About what, Salem? Stop joking around."

"Oh, I'm not trying to joke, Mala. I'm serious. I used to hear stories from fisherman at the ports of *Zambo*. Tales of the monsters attacking them at night," I whisper slyly, "The blood-sucking, man-eating vampire!"

Mala shakes their head as if disagreeing with the story and trying their best not be scared of the tale.

"They say that during the day it disguises itself as an older, beautiful woman," I change my voice to cultivate a menacingly dramatic tone, "But at night it severs its own upper torso and turns into a demon with bat-like wings, and they lure men and eat their hearts out of their bodies. They say their favorite meal is unsuspecting sleeping women, especially those who are pregnant."

Mala shivers, "Why pregnant women?"

"Think about it, it's like a two for one deal."

Mala's whole body starts trembling as they turn away from me to stare into the ocean trying to avoid picturing it, "What a vicious and evil monster."

An opportunity! I think to myself. I creep slowly behind them, their poor, unsuspecting soul. I let out a loud screech from behind, grabbing Mala's shoulders and shaking them.

"AHH!" Mala screams. They push me off them and make a bitter face as I laugh. "Not funny at all, Salem!"

At first, they're angry but Mala manages to roll their eyes and laugh back.

"Oh, come on, I couldn't help it. Learn to take a joke, will you?" I say as I walk back to the *vinta*'s stern and begin to paddle again. "It's just a fairy tale anyways, nothing to be afraid of. I'm here to protect you. You trust me right, *Ading*?"

"I trust you."

CHAPTER 5

CASTAWAY

Mala

Nightfall has come, and our adventure to follow the *Takay Flower* Constellation continues. I see Salem standing, his tall and sturdy demeanor, continuing to paddle the *vinta* as we sail toward the North Star. It is another long night, but we are both well-rested from relaxing during the day.

There's nothing like the feeling of the cold air of the ocean winds lightly cooling my body as I huddle under the blanket. Sitting by the lamp, I feel the warmth of the fire. I hear the sounds of the waves lapping below us. The water is kind to us, rocking the *vinta*, but never enough to feel dangerous. As I touch the waves, I feel the energy of incoming fish moving underwater. Always on the move, they sing a tireless song of constant swimming. It makes me want to swim with them—to dip into the water and feel the rush of their never-ending motion.

With another long night, I am lost in my own thoughts as it seems to be the only way to pass time. I can't help but think of the monster that Salem mentioned earlier. *If deities were real, then wouldn't creatures like the Manananggal be real too?* I shiver at the thought of such a creature.

I remember what *Sidapa* had said back at the forest—how he warned me about the strong magic of the island and the dangers that we cannot see. *Would we be strong enough to protect ourselves on this quest, much less fight the Bakunawa... the Moon Eater?* I really can only glow, and Salem isn't a fully recognized warrior. *I wonder if his training has been enough.*

Again, my doubts and worries take the better of my mind. I need to relax and clear my thoughts. I close my eyes and immerse myself in the atmosphere of my surroundings, allowing the rocking of the *vinta* to gently put me at peace. Rocking with the motion of the *vinta* as it drifts afloat feels wonderful. *Floating.* Yes, floating objects allow themselves to be carried by the current. I start to imagine that feeling, allowing my insides to feel like a river once again and let the energy flow inside of me.

I feel better. At least for a while. With my eyes still closed, I see only darkness and feel the ocean surrounding me. My body no longer feels heavy, but quite light as if I am one with the air— free and detached from the anchor of the Earth. *What a strange feeling*, I think to myself. Then I open my eyes.

I realize I was no longer on the *vinta*; I am above it. I see myself, or rather, my physical body, sitting still and with its eyes closed. And there is Salem paddling the boat. This dimension is not grounded, but also isn't a dream. No, it can't be—the abstract nature of this realm and experience is unlike anything I have known before. "*Kuya!*" I yell, but Salem does not respond. I look at my hands and this time I am glowing the silver light from before, except my body is entirely transparent. A dream would have been much better than whatever this is. My essence continues to float upward into the clouds as I look at myself become smaller, floating farther and farther away into the clouds. *How am I floating right now?*

"*Ku ku ku,*" an eerie voice echoes in the air. *Is it laughter?* I can't tell where it is coming from.

Because of the dark of the night, I can only see a vast crater of clouds form below me. The navy, sheet-like clouds shroud the sky, like a sea of fluffy cotton. In the openness of the midnight sky, I feel the pressure of the high altitude. Even in this spiritual state, my soul is still able to feel the energy of nature. I listen to the wind howl and to the waves of the seas. I feel the passing vibrations of birds flying by at a distance. *This must be why birds fly all the time. The view is magnificent. To think I can fly—Salem will never believe this.* The Moon's shining beauty is as clear as day; the lunar glow gleams magnificently. *It almost looks full. Yes, the lunar eclipse is almost upon us,* I remind myself.

Only emptiness in the darkness at first, and then the voice returns.

"*Ku ku ku,*" it echoes in the air, but this time it is followed by what looks to be a bright light slowly approaching, the *Takay Flower* Constellation gleaming right behind it. *Is it a star?* Then, as the light approaches, so does the being—its embodied being—a spirit walking above in the clouds like the sky is her walkway. Her pompous strut is revered with each stride as confident as the last.

She is a beautiful woman who looks to be older than I, but still youthful. Her body is radiating but isn't translucent like mine. Her brown skin is reminiscent of the earth, clay crafted in perfection. Her attire is so colorful and stimulating to my eyes. She wears a black-beaded dress, the beads like pearls dyed black; how they glisten. She wears a corset varnished in emerald and her shoulders hold a golden shawl made of silk that wraps around her neck and drapes down her body. An array of flowers like vineyards wrap around her forehead like a headpiece. She wears a beaded necklace and a beautiful golden amulet reflecting the Moon's silver light. Her energy feels grounded and firm, like the Earth, though she stands here, floating in the sky. She reminds me of the symphonies of nature, the trees, and the soil. *Remarkable.*

"*Ku ku ku*, hello dear child. We finally meet."

"What…is this place?"

"This place is this place," she says, simply.

I shake my head in confusion, "No I mean, is this a dream?"

"We are here in real time in the physical realm. Our consciousness, however, has assumed an existence outside of our physical body, traveling so we may meet freely without the bounds of and limitations of distance. This is what is known as 'astral projection.'"

"How—How are we doing this right now?"

"Well, I called you over. Simple as that! I felt your spiritual energy close to my island."

"Island?" I pause and realize what she means. "Wait, are you from the *Isla Sirena*?"

"Yes, my dear, home to the mysterious otherworld of magic and the unknown."

"You must be a *Babaylan* then!" I say excitedly, "It's my first-time meeting one. I've been looking for you!"

"In the astral flesh," she bows. "And I have been expecting you, as well. A pleasure to meet another strong shaman like myself."

"You've been looking for me too? You must know about the prophecy, then?" I ask. "And you must be mistaken, I am no shaman."

She nods. "Yes, the prophecy that must be fulfilled by the shaman chosen by the Moon. As the *Babaylan* of this island, I am very familiar with the history of the Great Battle of Moons that took place at the Enchanted Lake. With the upcoming lunar eclipse, I have felt the dangers of the Blood Moon grow near." She begins to wave her hand. With one swipe of her arm, the sky changes its hue from the admiral blue to a blood red that drips in the night sky. With another swipe of her hand, she returns the sky to its normal blue hue.

"A glimpse of what I had seen from my divination," she says. "The lunar eclipse is near, but we have an upper-hand. You, my dear, the lunar legacy, are a strong caster—a shaman who can produce sorcery from what you can feel and see."

"Sorcery...as in actual magic?"

"*Ku ku ku*, you ask many questions for our chosen champion."

"I'm sorry, I was never aware of my gifts until recently. Everything has been moving so fast," I say, "but if I am so strong, why am I having trouble controlling my powers?"

"Energy is tied to your emotional state, my dear. You mustn't let the flow of your connection be stopped by mental blockages. Don't worry, in due time, I will teach you. The talent in you is inherent. It is about controlling what has awakened within your destiny."

"Yes, that makes sense! I have so many questions," I say. Before I can go on, I detect an unusual sound breaking the calm flow of the ocean waves and air—energy in the air like no other.

My ears begin to ring. "Arghhh!" I yell as I cover my ears. The vibration waves feel far, but forthcoming, still loud, and rowdy.

The woman gives off a concerned expression. I can tell the *Babaylan* has felt it too. "It looks like we do not have much time to speak. You must make haste back to your ship, my dear," she warns. "And meet me on the shores of my home once you arrive."

I feel my essence begin to sink below the clouds like an anchor being pulled back to the boat. Before I lose sight of the woman, I yell out, "Wait! What is your name!"

"*Ate Lanie*," her voice echoed in the air, "Remember, you must let the energy flow inside you!"

I hear this final message as my astral essence is dragged back to my body and its darkness until I wake up.

I take a huge gasp of air, exhaling deeply as my consciousness returns to my body back on the *vinta*. I feel revived in my own flesh, even though I was only away from it for a few moments.

Salem had rushed over to check on me. "Mala, are you okay? Was it another dream?"

I take a few heavy breaths and touch my necklace, thinking of Mother to calm myself. I feel my sweat drip down from my face. My body is heavy again and tired, not used to the physical strain that comes from channeling out-of-body escapades.

"I think my soul just projected into the sky," I tell him.

"Well...that's a first," says Salem, "What happened?"

"I met this *Babaylan* from the *Isla Sirena*. Her name is *Ate Lanie*. She said she could sense my energy closing into the island. We must be close."

Salem looks out into the ocean and squints his eyes. He shakes his head. "It's still too dark for me to see anything, but we should see the island by daybreak."

My muscles begin to relax, and my head feels heavy and dizzy, as if my soul and body are not completely realigned yet.

But then I feel it, the clamorous vibration. I close my eyes to concentrate on this strange disruption of energy, but my mind is still frazzled. I can tell the direction of the rapid vibration in the air. I look at the *Takay Flower* Constellation and realize the energy I am sensing is coming from that direction and must be originating from the *Isla Sirena*.

The cascading motion grows closer. Its beats feel like large wings flapping in the sky, creating ricochets in the natural course of the ocean air.

"Something is coming," I warn as I look over to Salem, "I felt its energy while my consciousness was drifting afloat."

"What, where? I can't see too well." He grabs the lamp and runs over to meet me in the front of the *vinta*. He holds it into the air, the fire of the lamp shimmers softly in the quiet.

"Do you hear that?" I ask

"Yeah, it sounds like...large flapping? Is something flying toward us?" asks Salem.

Darkness shrouds our view, but I can feel it—its immense vibration blasting noisily in the air. In the shadows of the darkness, a monstrous face emerges in the light, its blood-shot eyes glaring and long fang-filled mouth wide open. We hear a demonic screech,

"*AAEERRCHHHHHHH!*"

The flap of the beast's wings creates a large gust as it flies over above us, causing us to fall backwards into the *vinta*. The lamp drops to the floorboard. The beating of the creature's wings is so strong that it creates large waves that rock the *vinta*. Salem and I grab the mast of the sail so that we do not fly overboard.

"What is that?" he yells.

The loud, bat-like beast flaps its wings, with each screech causing my ears to ring. "Arrrgh," I say as I cover my ears. Quickly, I maneuver to grab the lamp and shine it bright on the demon in the sky. It looks to only have an upper torso and pale, hairless skin that stretches throughout the tip of its wings and claws. The bottom half of it is missing, allowing the beast to be agile in flight.

Bat-like wings...an upper torso demon? "It's a *Manananggal!*" I scream.

"No...no way," Salem says as he stares at it, stunned. The fables and legends of this creature used to scare us as kids in the night. To see it now, alive and ready to be its next meal, strikes terror though my whole body. They are strong creatures that even groups of warriors have trouble facing together. They can kill hundreds of men, women, and children in their lifetime, leaving a blood bath whenever it visited a village or city. Salem doesn't move. His body is still as stone.

The *Manananggal* swipes a long, whip-like tongue, its tip like a spear and drenched in crimson flesh.

"Salem, move! Now!" I yell—but he can't move, stunned at the creature's blood-thirsty glare.

It wastes no time, eager to strike its prey like a skilled predator. Its long tongue shoots like a dart, aiming at Salem's heart.

"NO!" I shout and, without hesitation, throw the lamp in front of Salem.

The beast's tongue makes contact with the glass, breaking the lamp. The oil and fire combust from the impact. The fire and oil mixes with the vampire's demonic flesh, recoiling its deadly appendage back into its mouth.

Salem finally snaps out of his trance. Immediately, he prepares his bow and arrow, aiming it at the *Manananggal*—now in clear sight. Its large tongue flickers from the scorching blaze. Its loud screeches ring in the quiet of the night. I feel it too, the pain from the fire burning of its tongue. *Wait can I feel this creature's pain—how is this possible? Maybe this creature is just like any spirit.*

With a single breath, Salem shoots his arrow. The arrow flies perfectly and makes direct contact, hitting the demon in the head then plummeting into the murky waters.

We both breathe deeply, exhausted after the wicked encounter.

"I thought those things were just stories...myths! I used to have nightmares about that thing," Salem sighs.

"I felt it's aura. It's as real and alive as any deadly preda-tor—like a shark or a crocodile, except it dominates the air."

"Yeah and eats people! Unlike a shark or crocodile, humans are its main source of food. The hunter becomes the hunted. Not a good look for me, *Ading*. I was lucky enough to shoot it down with my long bow *pana*," says Salem.

"We must be close to the *Isla Sirena*. *Sidapa* warned that the island has strong magic and powerful creatures. I told you, it will be a dangerous quest."

"Well, it's lucky for you that you have a *Kuya* who is a great shot and saved the day," Salem boasts.

I want to smile and agree, but something still feels off. *Is the monster really dead?* It is hard to tell with the motion of the fish and the water's waves. I can't concentrate to pinpoint the beast's energy under the water.

"In your stories, how does a *Manananggal* usually die?" I ask.

"Well, I've only heard of them being killed if the upper torso of its body doesn't get back to its bottom half by daybreak."

My heart sinks. *It must still be alive under the water.* The vibrations of the waves begin to ricochet from beneath the *vinta*. The malevolent vampire darts out of the water, climbs on the side of the *vinta*, and appears right behind Salem. Salem turns around, attempting to grab his sword, but is too slow. With its devilish claws, the *Manananggal* grabs Salem, spreads its wings, and takes him in to the air—screeching like an eagle catching its prey.

"Mala!" he yells, trying to fight of beast midair.

This demon is going to kill my brother! My mind goes blank. The fear I have vanishing, only a sense of urgency to save my brother fills my head. Overwhelmed, I motion my hands in the air. A loud rumble shakes through the sky, activating something in me and my new resolve awakens. It feels like a locked gate opened within me, drawing power from the Moon and commanding the tides. A strong, violent rush of energy flows within me. I am unable to control this rush of power. I look down and see my body glowing vibrant with a familiar silver luminescence.

I reach out toward my brother, trying to reach him as he flies away. Suddenly, as I reach my hands out, I feel the flow of energy from within me blast outward. A large wall of water blasts upward, reaching the clouds of the sky. *Did I create that?* The wall of water closes off the flight path, preventing the *Manananggal* from flying away. *This must be sorcery.* The demon continues to screech, and my brother continues to try to fight off the bat-like monster.

"Salem!" I yell out, clenching my fist, controlling the shape of the wall of water. The force of pressure increases, causing the wall of water to close in onto the *Manananggal*. The creature drops Salem, and he plummets into the ocean. The water wall crashes down, creating a tsunami that pushes the *vinta* over. I get knocked out of the boat with the collision.

I fall into the depths of the water. All I can see is darkness and feel the coldness of the waves surround me.

CHAPTER 6

FRUIT OF LIFE

———

Mala

I awaken and am no longer on the *vinta* sailing the ocean waters. I recall being submerged fully in the waters of the ocean, the cold tides clutching my entire body as I sank into the depths. I clutch my necklace, my mother's pearls still lined around my neck.

Where is Salem?

I look around and he is nowhere to be seen. Instead, I only see that I am in a room made of wood, the roots of the tree sprouted amongst the textile floors. The roof is covered in branches and deep green foliage, shrouding every corner and the top of the walls. I see a soft light from the windows, a faint haze. *It must be morning.*

I remember being attacked by the vicious *Mananang-gal. Was it another dream? More like a nightmare. No, it had to have been real, but where am I now?*

Jars of spices and concoctions are lying all around the small room. I look out of the door to see a trail of smoke sneaking inside, followed by the scent of spices, sulfur, and mud. I inhale deeply the aroma, clearing my head and soothing my lungs. It pulls me to my feet, and I follow the smell and trail of smoke.

Outside I am greeted by a *bukaw*[22] that flies toward me, flapping its large wings loudly as it makes its way to perch itself on a miniature tree growing from a ground spot on the corner of the room. The *bukaw's* feathers are coated in bronze orange, like the shade of dusk, while it's chest and belly are white. It stares at me with a reverent silence, its honey eyes giving off an energy of peace—like a chime that is ringing and reverberating throughout my body, clearing my mind. Its notes of beauty show it's a mindful and attentive character.

I look over to the side and see Salem. He is sitting on a seat next to a wooden table in the middle of the room. On the table lie three unlit candles and a knife. My pouch is also there, on top of the table. *The copperplate!* I rush toward it and open my bag to see the copperplate still there. I pull it out and place it on the table, relieved to not have lost it in the ocean.

"You're awake, *Ading!*" says Salem, grinning beside me, as if we didn't just nearly escape the dangers of a *Manananggal*.

A woman suddenly enters the room. It is the woman from my astral dream on the *vinta*! *"Ate Lanie!"* I yell. She looks just like she did during our meeting in the navy night sky, her vibrant nature fills the room. She carries carabao mangoes in her hands.

"Ku ku ku, I am pleased to see both of you children awake! Sorry for the smell, I have been cooking up some remedies in the kitchen. But here, you must eat. These are the native fruits we grow on our island," she says as she places the mangoes in front of us.

---

22 Bukaw – Eagle-owl endemic to the Philippines

"*Salamat!*" I say.

"Yes, *Maraming Salamat*," Salem says too, grabbing the knife and cutting the mango in half. "Here," he says, handing the other half of the mango to me. *So sweet!* I think to myself as I bite into the mango. It's delicious, fresh juices fill my mouth.

Ate Lanie joins us, sitting on the other side of the table with an angelic smile.

I finish eating my mango and words start spilling out of my mouth. "How did we get here? Where are we?"

"Yeah, one moment we were fighting off a bat monster, and then the next thing I remember I plunged down into the ocean waters!" laughs Salem.

"Well, you both have finally arrived at the *Isla Sirena*. After our astral meeting in the skies with the chosen lunar legacy," she says as she looks at me, "I, too, felt a strange disturbance in the air. I was concerned, so I brought a group of warriors from this kingdom to watch over the shores of the island as we awaited your arrival. We saw a bright glowing light from a distance and then watched a great, massive wall of water emerge to the heavens."

"Yes, I remember. I felt the power of the Moon surge within me. I think I created that wall of water."

"Yes, you did. That is sorcery, my dear. Your powers are finally being awakened," she says, "and it is what saved you and your *Kuya*'s lives!"

The energy flowed inside of me. This time I allowed it, the Moon's lunar power rushed through me like an uncontrollable river and I projected it out as a wall of water.

"I, along with the warriors of our kingdom, got on our ships and headed toward the light. We were able to save you both and even salvaged your boat. We brought you and your belongings back here, to the Kingdom of *Taal*, our home on this island."

Kingdom of Taal? I have never heard of such a place in readings or maps.

"And what happened to the *Manananggal*?" inquires Salem.

"The demon seemed to have disappeared in the ocean once the warriors and I arrived. Our people are grateful to you both for handling the demon. It has been attacking the kingdom for quite some time now, and we have not been successful in fighting it off."

"You're my hero," Salem says, playfully nudging my head with his hands.

"We were just lucky," I say.

"Auspicious…indeed. Fate brought you both, and you are here now, to the *Isla Sirena* as I had seen in my divination. Two brave souls to tackle the incoming Blood Moon Eclipse."

The eclipse is approaching! "Yes, we need to find the Mask of Gold. The prophecy foretells it to be in the Enchanted Lake. I met *Sidapa* and he said I must go see the *Nagas* who guard those waters. They must be protecting the mask."

"The Deity of Death, wonderful," *Ate Lanie* said, "Yes, I have encountered the God of Death many times on this island in the Enchanted Lake. How he longs to see his lover again."

"*Bulan*," I finish.

She nods, "I will help you on your quest to go to the Enchanted Lake, but for now you will both be safe here in the Kingdom of *Taal*. Before we make our way to the Enchanted Lake, you must take a day to rest and build up your energy. I know the travel through the ocean was long and tiring."

Salem gets up from his seat and yells, "Isn't the next eclipse just three nights from now? We have no time to rest!" as he slams his hands on the table.

"You must not undermine the power of rest, young warrior," she says. *How did she know Salem is a warrior? She must be a powerful Babaylan to be able to have such a keen perception.*

"*Ate Lanie* is right, *Kuya*," I say, "I still feel drained from our last encounter with the *Manananggal*; we barely made it out alive."

Salem sits back down and takes a deep breath, trying to calm his fuse. I know he is just as worried as I am. The stakes are too high, and we don't have much time. "I want to learn more about *Ate Lanie* and about being a *Babaylan*. I need to understand how to grow stronger with this newfound power," I tell him.

"I see you have a temper in you that needs to be tamed," she says to Salem, "Anger is a most powerful emotion, but letting it consume you will not save you in the end. You must find a path to enlightenment and find a way to let out your frustrations in order to rest properly."

Salem sulks but then says, "I am open to finding a new way. Just like Mala, I need to learn to grow, too. What do you suggest, *Ate Lanie*?"

"Why don't you take a stroll throughout our kingdom? Outside my home, past the rice paddies, is the entrance to the City of *Jati*, the capital of our kingdom. You may meet the *Taal* warriors that saved you and your *Ading*. I suggest learning more about our warriors' way. They may offer you some clarity," she suggests.

"Warriors? Count me in!" Salem shouts excitedly as he gets up from his seat and begins to leave, "Mala will you be okay if I head out?"

"Oh, I have a feeling we will see you soon," says *Ate Lanie*, smiling.

Salem makes a puzzled face at her response, but I nod my head, "I'll be okay, *Kuya*. We can meet you later."

Salem gives me another rub on the head with his fist before heading out to explore the City of *Jati*.

"I know you must feel restless, too. We are on borrowed time, but you must not rush your process, Mala. Be okay with slowing down, and the stars will align to your true destiny," she says.

I want to trust *Ate Lanie*'s words, but the thought of the lunar eclipse approaching so soon and of the dangers of the *Bakunawa* fills my thoughts. I start to feel quite disheartened. *Can we do anything at all to stop her from eating the Moon?*

Ate Lanie gives me a heartfelt look. She gets up from her seat and begins to dance around the room, trying her best to uplift and relieve the tension in the air. As I watch her dance, I see the *bukaw* staring as well, rhythmically moving its head to the beat of *Ate Lanie*'s movements. Each step was an elegant float, her polished gestures evoking a strong energetic wave in the air.

"We are shamans, my dear, *Babaylans*, to be exact!" *Ate Lanie* proudly noted. "We must believe in our power," she celebrates as she claps her hands together rhythmically.

I can't help but smile and soon we are dancing. Her energy is infectious, and my body begins to dance, too. *I wish I could free my mind of my worries, the way that she can.*

Then, she stops. With a dramatic snap of her fingers, she lights fire on the three candles on the table. The fire burns brightly and reminds me of when *Sidapa* had done the same with my branch. *Wow, is this sorcery, as well?*

She walks back toward the table, and I join her. The mood of the air changes from whimsical to reflective. She lightly circles her hands above the candles, the wisps of the fire pulling and moving with each motion of her wrist, like pulling strings on a puppet. "In the great art of alchemy and healing, the fire does the work. The fire is the medium. We put our faith in the fire to purify, to create, to heal, and most importantly, to guide our community. This magic is not simply given but earned through trust. I draw my power to create what is produced in nature."

The way *Ate Lanie* talks about fire makes me feel less alone. She can feel it too, the energy of the burn. It is more than just heat and light. I wonder, though, how she is able to produce this type of sorcery. "From where do you draw your power?" I ask.

"As you draw power from the Moon, I draw my power from the earth—or, more specifically, I call to the *Mother Lakapati*,[23] Deity of Fertility and Agriculture. Through her power and blessings, I am able to create. This is my sorcery, whether it's creating potions for the sick or blessing the land with rice, crops, and fruits for a harvest throughout the seasons. I sometimes rely on fire for these purposes and practices, as well."

So this is a Babaylan. Her powers are used to help the people in times of need. I am fascinated, "Can you tell me more about the Deity Lakapati?"

"My relationship with *Lakapati* begins with my journey to becoming a *Babaylan*," she says. She brushes her long silky hair and gets lost in her own thoughts for a moment. I stare at her pensive face as she seems to reminisce about her past days, "Long ago, I was given the opportunity to be very close to the previous *Babaylan* of *Taal* and studied her

---

23   Lakapati – Deity of Fertility & Agriculture; known for her kindness amongst all the other Deities; Transgender Deity and protector of fields

ways of practice. I was always in awe, watching her divine work as she healed the people from sickness and provided care through childbirth. Her participation in the ceremonies were blessings to the tribe and our kingdom. A miracle, as many used to say."

"So *Babaylans* are like healers for the community?" I ask.

"Yes!" she exclaims, "It has been the most fulfilling work to know that the community depends on our spiritual practices."

"That sounds beautiful. How did you become connected with the previous *Babaylan*?" I ask. *Was she drawn to her magical energy the way I was drawn to the energy of the copperplate?*

She takes a deep breath and starts to play with one of the fires from the candle. The fires dance between her fingers until the flames begin to change shape to form a small human body. "I was born the child of the *Datu*,[24] one of the leaders who ruled a given city within the Kingdom of *Taal*. My father was the *Datu* for the Capital, the City of *Jati*, which is right near my home. He reports to the *Lakan*[25]—our King who resides in our capital, as well. When I was younger, my father raised me as a son, though I had always felt like a daughter."

I want to be a sister and a daughter, too, sometimes. If Mother had lived, would she have treated me like her daughter and not just as a son? I thought. I begin to see myself in *Ate Lanie*. I recognize her journey to becoming the lively and powerful *Babaylan* woman of this island.

Ate Lanie continues to play with her fire figurines. Like puppets, she creates characters out of the fire, showcasing a display of her story. "The shaman before me," *Ate Lanie*

---

24 Datu – Chief of City or Village
25 Lakan – Paramount ruler; equivalent to Rajah or King

continues to say, "was another powerful elder woman and was always around the *Datu* at the time, working closely in his aid. There, my relationship with her blossomed. Most of the *Babaylans* who are chosen are women, at least in our community. The older teachings prove the power of femininity comes with divinity—that our belief of motherhood, fertility, and healing is tied to our spiritual embodiment of the bounty of the Earth," she says as she creates a maidenlike figure, her blaze dances beautifully across the wooden table. "You see, I was supposed to be a *Datu* after my father, but when I was younger, my desire and aspirations were to be like the shaman instead. She was celestial, like her being belonged with the stars alongside *Tala*, Deity of Stars, traveling along the endless night sky of the galaxy. Her power was magnifying. She recognized something within me one day and decided to train me once I was ready. She then introduced me to *lakas*."[26]

"*Lakas*?"

"*Lakas* is our strength, our power. In simple terms, it is the energy that exists within all of us, from the blaze of the fire I create to the auras we sense from living creatures. It is our life force."

It all begins to make sense. The energy and feelings of vibrations. It all comes from the power of our *lakas*. "So, everything has *lakas*?"

"Yes, all things that exist spiritual and physical carry *lakas* of some form. The energy is just different. As *Babaylans*, we have the power to feel, sense, and even channel this

---

26   Lakas – "Strength" in Tagalog; it is the spiritual/magical energy, power, lifeforce of this world

energy. As you find out, it is different from being to being, but still exists."

"Why is that?"

"Because our *lakas*, the energy, can change. You see, *lakas* cannot be used fully. They are only borrowed, the flow of our lifeforce lives on through new forms and can be converted, manipulated or transformed."

"That is why they always feel different!"

"Yes, and we *Babaylans* harness and manipulate *lakas* with our gifts. Each *Babaylan* has their own unique *lakas* power, as well. Our special *lakas* is rooted within our identity, our personal struggles and characteristics that make us, well... us! It then manifests from our inner truth, from what makes you different. Mine is the gift of creations that was bestowed upon me by *Lakapati*. Yours is the power from the Moon, bestowed to you from *Bulan*."

I start to feel excited about this power. I am learning so much from *Ate Lanie* about *lakas*. She empowers me, and I appreciate her wisdom. I want to know what the Moon meant for me—how my *lakas* differ from *Ate Lanie*'s power to create.

I wonder, too, if Lau would've trained me as well if things had turned out differently in *Zambo*. "So how did you know when you were ready?"

"Well, it wasn't easy. At first, I couldn't feel *lakas*. Not all are gifted or born with the ability, but once chosen, one can finally feel it. The road to becoming a *Babaylan* is different for everyone. For me, I had to come to terms with a challenge that was blocking my energy flow. I always tell you; you must let the energy flow inside you, but at the time something inside me was not in complete balance and harmony. Ever since I was young, I felt very different within my body."

I lean in toward the table, growing more engrossed by her words.

"At a young age, I knew I was not raised the way that I felt. At the time, though, I had no one to talk to, especially not my father," *Ate Lanie* shrivels at the thought but then proceeds to move her right hand, placing it on her heart. Her left hand creates a kneeling fire maiden, praying, "And that's when I called to *Lakapati* for guidance and prayed every night for a sign. At first there was no response, but one day," she says as she gestures her hand to create a small ball of fire in her palms, "I woke up to see a seed next to my pillow."

My eyes widened as she continued to tell her story, "A seed?"

"It was one I had never seen before, but I planted the seed in my house right there, in the corner were the *bukaw* lies perched. I cared for the seed each day and night. Finally, the seed sprouted, and it turned into a small tree. I wondered if it was a sign. I chose not to give up and continued to water the tree until I began to notice large roots sprouting from underneath the floors. Then, from those roots, more branches grew from and covered my home, the leaves creating a new roof of foliage above."

"So the small tree grew to be this protective shield over your home?"

She nods, "I slowly came to realize that the seed was connected to my spirit, and that its growth represented my self-love and protection. You see, the seed symbolized my rebirth and newfound strength. This daily discipline of self-love was one of *Lakapati*'s teachings for me. My *lakas* is the power of creation. She showed me that I am connected to the Earth like she is and that I have the ability to create—whether that's producing food through sorcery or preparing concoctions through alchemy. The mangoes that you ate this morning came from the same tree in my home."

I am amazed to hear this story. The power from Lakapati is marvelous and befitting for a kind and caring soul like Ate Lanie.

"I grew to love and learn about myself because of this tree. I had finally accepted my womanhood at an early age. That's when I knew I was ready to learn under the previous shaman's wing. Once I accepted my path to become a *Babaylan* and after years of training, I was able to hone my spiritual connection fully. My strong feminine energy is crucial to my connection with the spirits. As the *Babaylan* of *Taal*, I have used this power to take care of the people who never grow hungry because of my gift," *Ate Lanie* smiles gently.

I feel joy and happiness from hearing her story. I relate with *Ate Lanie* in so many ways. Her power comes from her living her truth. *Truth.* A powerful testimony, something that I have yet to accept fully about myself. *What is my truth?* I have always felt that my power pulls from both my masculine and feminine aspects. Each power of a shaman must have their own different origins, like *Ate Lanie.*

"I hope to one day be like you," I say, "the citizens of *Zambo* back at my home were quite cruel to me, but hearing your story gives me hope."

"*Ku Ku Ku*, my dear child, I know you will have the impact to create an endless web of connections so you will no longer feel disconnected, but instead be an anchor to all relationships. For you see, you are connected to the divine, just like I am. Our relationship with the physical and spiritual aspects of this world and other realms is our own inherent ability that allows us to communicate with any spirit. We must listen to the auras around us. We can connect to them like a bridge.

The better you learn to control your gift, a sturdier bridge you will become, creating bonds that will last many lifetimes."

Maybe my truth does not have to be my pain or what isolates me from others, but instead a hope that can bridge differences.

"Let us try and practice with my *Abyan*[27] friend here," she suggests, calling over the *bukaw*. The eagle owl flew from its nest flying around *Ate Lanie* and me, circling back to land on the table in front of me.

"*Abyan*?" I ask.

"An *Abyan* is known as a spirit guide. They act as our companions, but like any relationship, they have a right to choose to join in an *Abyan* pact with a *Babaylan*."

"Just like a friendship," I say.

"Exactly, chosen one! The friendship I have with the *bukaw* was earned and will be enduring for the remainder of my life. His name is *Kalma*. If you make a pact, their essence becomes tied to your spirit as yours becomes tied to theirs."

Making friends was always something that I struggled with growing up but knowing I can become friends with Abyans makes me so happy. But how can I connect with a bukaw? I look deeply into *Kalma*'s eyes and listen to the chiming noise again, clearing my mind. I close my eyes to concentrate on the vibration, "I can feel *Kalma*'s aura."

"A simple chime, yet a skillfully constructed tune that is firm. Can you try to match your energy with his wavelength?"

---

27   Abyan – Spirit guide; companion to Babaylans

But how? Then, I remember I need to be a bridge. I take a deep breath, and allow the chime projected from *Kalma* to flow inside my body. *Yes, I allow their spirit to cross over to mine, opening a channel of energy within me.* The chime's vibrations begin to feel intense and my body starts to slightly shake, overwhelmed by the external aura. His wavelengths start to take over.

"The *bukaw* are eagle owls that have lived on these islands for centuries and carry a wisdom from generation to generation within their spirits. It's a spirit that can see right through you, remember that. Calm your emotions and don't let your nerves take over."

I let *Ate Lanie*'s soothing voice guide me and I can see it, the clarity of vision and intellect that provides a deep insight and understanding of this world. I begin to feel more relaxed, more in control of my body and mind. I intake a heavy inhale and, as I exhale, I project the same chime, feeding the tune back to *Kalma*'s spirit. I feel it, the energy feedback loop between us beginning to tie us together.

"Aspects of femininity and masculinity exist in everyone. Wisdom shares this, as well. You must find a balance between both feminine and masculine qualities. Allow both energies to co-exist within you in harmony. Let *Kalma* be your teacher of masculinity, embrace his masculine wisdom and learn how it may be different from your femininity. The Moon is the bringer of balance. When you accept the balance within you, you will master the power of the Moon."

I listen to the chime of *Kalma*'s spirit flow with mine. At first it is hard to find a tune to match his, but once I concentrate my energy to understand his, it becomes easier to match his rhythm. Then, I start to listen carefully to *Kalma*'s chime. This time I start to absorb his wisdom. My entire body feels calm, as if his energy is relaxing my spirit. Masculinity is driven, assertive, and in control. But these characteristics do not distance themselves from my femininity. They are not absent of each other at all. These qualities just merely exist.

As I start to learn more about these traits, I begin to understand my gender identity better. These qualities are just factors that do not define my being. There is no push and pull of masculinity and femininity, but instead a natural flow, like tides of the ocean being pulled by the Moon. It is balanced and my gender is free to change based on my own feelings, agency, and expression. *That change is okay. There are no borders or rules that define my identity.* Neither of these qualities, feminine and masculine, take away from each other. They both just exist within me as they exist within everything, like a beautiful harmony. The root of balance is freedom.

I open my eyes and stare back at *Kalma* who gazes wonderfully at me with his honey-yellow eyes. With my right hand, I reach out to touch *Kalma*, but he suddenly opens his wings and flies from above the table, circling around the room and landing right on my shoulder. I look back to see *Ate Lanie* nodding in approval.

"You are a natural, my dear! Now you have made an *Abyan* pact with *Kalma*, as well. He is a spirit guide that will help to give you clarity when you are in need," she proclaims.

I understand now what *Ate Lanie* means. *Kalma* chose me—he accepts me for who I am just as much as I accept him for all he is. I am grateful for this newfound friendship, and I have a lot to learn from *Kalma*'s wisdom. I must learn to harness this new technique.

I sigh in relief, "That was tough, I have never tried to create a bond with another spirit before, nor have I tried to actually befriend one. If I had learned to do this before, I wouldn't have felt so alone back in *Zambo*."

"That is one of the true powers of being a shaman. We build bridges and create spiritual relationships with those around us."

"Yes, *Ate Lanie*, it means the world to me to have an older sister like you to help guide me through all of this," I say gratefully. Her gentle nature and tenderness are so delightful. It is the sisterly relationship I have always dreamed of having.

She gets up from her table and gives me a hug. Her warm presence and scent of sage is serene.

"I am most honored to hear this from our champion. Now, I believe we must go to see the *Lakan*."

CHAPTER 7

PRINCESS OF *TAAL*

Salem

Leaving *Ate Lanie*'s home, I look behind and see the outside of the hut engrossed by branches and leaves, the walls inter-twined with trunks of several trees. Outside of her home, we are surrounded by a cultivation of rice crops, the pre-husk green grasses sprouting above the wet watery mud. The rice terraces of this land are vast, each series of flat areas made on a slope that looked like several hills, the agricultural design was unlike any I have seen before. Back in *Zambo*, our city relied heavily on fishing and hunting—we had grown crops, but never on a large scale like this.

I continue to walk the muddy pathway of the rice paddies that leads me to see the outskirts of the Kingdom of *Taal* from a hilltop viewpoint. The kingdom is vast and can fit many cities, it looked to be three times the size of the City of *Zambo*. I take in the view and reminisce about the scenery of *Zambo*, what I used to see from above at the Temple of Serpents. I start to feel nervous. *Maybe I should've waited back at the hut for Mala.* But I have always been an explorer. Ever since I was young, I was unafraid of leaving home to venture into the forest and waters as a hunter. I befriended the fishermen of *Zambo* and impressed them with my natural skills of the hunt. *How hard could it be to make some friends in a new place? I could surely impress the Taal warriors with my own skills and trainings, too.*

I walk down the slope of the rice hills and enter the passage into the city. The homes remind me of my own home in *Zambo*, except these huts are much larger and fortified throughout the city. The huts could fit a family of five or six and are made of bamboo. The rooftops are covered and layered in straw.

The streets of the city are busy, much like the heavy crowds of the *Zambo* market. The people of *Taal* have golden bronze skin, luscious dark hair, and deep, dark-colored eyes. Here, the men wear splendid red pants and tops. The women wear robe-like dresses of different shades of violet, blue, and coral. They look to be made of silk—colorful woven works of art. Interestingly, some of the men wear these robes, as well, and some of the women also wear the splendid red pants and tops. The garments of these clothes contain a variety of geometric designs and wrap around their bodies beautifully. The citizens of *Jati* all wear golden necklaces and bracelets. They also wear gold chains across their chests.

I notice a woman walking alone in my direction. Her face is striking and immediately catches my attention through the crowds of people surrounding us. She wears gold ornaments around her arms and neck; her gold tiara shines the brightest of her jewelry, holding her black hair in a bun-style look. The woman is beautiful. Her sun-kissed, dark, bronze skin glistens in the sun's glowing rays. She wears a magnificent golden-yellow silk dress that looks expensive compared to the rest of the gowns of the village women. She wears a deep velvet red corset that seems to be made of silk on top of her dress. She also wears shoulder pads. On her arms and legs are tattoos. *Is this woman a foreigner like me?*

I gulp. I feel sweat accumulating on my skin. My nerves begin, like butterflies fluttering in my stomach. I have never felt this way around a woman before.

She notices me right away and stops in her movements. She smiles graciously, "Hello, there. You must be one of the foreigners the people have been speaking about. Quite the gossip you have inspired around city."

I stammer a greeting, "H-hello, I'm Salem from *Zambo*."

The woman comes closer. She grabs my shaking hands, and her warm touch soothes my nerves. "I'm Princess Nadya of the Kingdom of *Taal*," she greets, "but you can just call me Nadya. Welcome to our capital, the City of *Jati*."

Princess!

Before I can say anything, the princess notes, "My warriors told me there were two of you. Where's the other one, your sister, I believe?"

"Sister? Oh, that's my *Ading*, Mala," I say. "They're actually with *Ate Lanie* back in her home."

Nadya looks back at the village and turns to me. "Would you care to join me?"

"Of course," I blush.

As we walk the city streets, Nadya speaks about the great Kingdom of *Taal* and about its expansion throughout the islands. I listen to the sound of her voice, mighty and strong, resonating with the fiery passion of her spirit as she excitedly talks about her people. I can tell she loves her kingdom. It is reassuring to see a spark of light in her eyes that makes the city feel less alienating. I feel the same passion and honor for the citizens of *Zambo*.

I learn of Nadya's family lineage. She is the daughter of *Lakan Ravi*, the King of *Taal*. "My father is a tough man, but that is what makes him a strong king and leader. I learn a lot from him."

I notice the citizens of *Jati* seem to be in high spirits, as well. Nadya's dominance rumbles the busy streets, yet the people are not afraid of her. Instead, they smile at her, bowing and tipping their heads to show respect. I notice some musicians playing drums and music from wooden instruments. The children playfully dance around, beating pots and pans and making loud noises. They sing songs unfamiliar to my ears, but are beautiful and friendly, nonetheless. My body slowly moves to the beat of the music.

I notice Nadya watching me as she starts to move to the rhythm of the songs, too. She smiles and spins in place, her feet fluttering over the ground as she joins the children in their playful dance. I watch in awe at the liveliness and beauty of the princess and her people. Nadya gestures me to come and join. *Me? I can't dance at all.* I shake my head at first, but soon I am pulled into her dance. The citizens from the nearest corners all join in to celebrate with us, playing their music and beating their pots and pans like drums. My feet follow the flow of the drums. I watch Nadya, closely moving with her and clapping along to the song.

Then, Nadya's mighty grip pulls me out of the dance circle. *She's strong*, I think to myself leaving the gathering.

"Your people are so energetic in the streets, is there a celebration happening tonight?" I ask.

"My people are preparing for the sacred Blood Moon Festival with the upcoming lunar eclipse. In our traditions, we play music and make loud noises, banging our pots and metal objects to ward off the *Bakunawa* dragon from eating the Moon during the eclipse," she says. "But *Ate Lanie* has warned us of her divination—That this year's Blood Moon may be our final one and that our faith is not strong enough to protect the Deity *Bulan* this time."

The people of Taal protect themselves from the Bakunawa. I feel guilty and remember that I almost swore an oath to become a Blood Moon Knight. *I need to warn the princess.*

"Yes, that's why Mala and I came here. We know of the prophecy! We have the key to stopping *Bakunawa*."

The princess' demeanor shifts, a serious tone projects as she looks upward to the sky. "The prophecy. Yes, our island's champion—the lunar legacy. We have waited years for them to return."

Return? She must mean return the copperplate inscription to the Enchanted Lake. "It's my *Ading*, Mala, they're the one of whom you speak. We have lived in *Zambo* all our lives but have ventured all the way here to see the prophecy through. I came to help."

"You are a great *Kuya*, very honorable," she says, and I blush.

"*Salamat*, Nadya. We need to go to the Enchanted Lake now and retrieve the Mask of Gold," I say with urgency, "That's why I left to come into the city. I wanted to find some warriors of *Taal* and convince them to leave with us tonight. Do you think you can lend us some warriors?"

Nadya squints her eyes and gives me an inquisitive look, "No," she says sternly. "At least not for tonight. As much as I admire your eagerness, I cannot just lend a foreigner my warriors, even if they are a part of the prophecy. As princess I need to make sure we take the right course of action."

I sigh deeply and recall *Ate Lanie* saying "no." I can hear her *ku ku ku* laugh, knowing she is right. I respect Nadya's decision. *She is a leader after all.* "I understand," I say, "But can I ask what is stopping us from just going to the Enchanted Lake?"

"Remember the creature that attacked you and your *Ading* that caused you to shipwreck?"

"Yes, the *Manananggal*?" I say.

"Well, the *Manananggal* is not the only beast that resides on this island. To get to the Enchanted Lake, we must travel east, outside the City of *Jati*, into the Forest of Lost Ones that lies outside of the Kingdom of *Taal*."

"Forest of Lost Ones. Why is it named that?"

"The area is ruled by the Beast King, the *Tikbalang*.[28] He is the keeper of the forest on this island and has protected it from wandering souls who seek to hurt it. Anyone who dares to trespass will be tricked by the *Tikbalang*'s power that leads them astray, lost in the forest forever."

"Why does the Beast King feel the need to protect the forest from you?"

"It's not us. The *Tikbalang* used to be a benevolent guardian of the forest. We used to pray at the Enchanted Lake, as it was our most sacred land on this entire island. Ever since the first Blood Moon eclipse, though, our island has never been the same. The recent invasions of the Blood Moon Knights—their attempts to conquer our land and resources—have disrupted the balance of nature causing the

---

28   Tikbalang – Bipedal horse creature that dwells in mountains and forests; native to the Philippines; Beast King; Keeper of the Forest of Lost Ones

Beast King to distrust humans. This is why we have been seeing recent attacks from creatures like the *Mananang-gal* who seek to hunt and hurt humans. The *Tikbalang* has allowed it."

"That makes sense. I'm sorry for even suggesting we leave so soon without a plan."

She places her hand on her heart, "As princess of this kingdom, I want to protect my people no matter what. But I also acknowledge that we are not the only rulers of this island. I respect the *Tikbalang* and hope to one day bring harmony to our tribes."

I look at Princess Nadya, staring into her eyes. For a moment, I am lost in them. Her dark brown irises almost look golden in the reflection of the sun. I can't help but feel her magnetic presence and powerful aura drawing me toward her. *Why do I feel this way?* I start to question, *Is it because I deeply admire her? The way she leads as royalty is so honorable. She not only cares about people, but about the magical inhabitants of this island.*

"Princess Nadya!" a loud voice interrupts our leisurely stroll. I turn around to see two warrior women dressed in their red cloth and golden-clad armor. They show more skin than the other citizens, revealing tattoos that look just like Nadya's. I have never seen warrior women before—the Blood Moon Knights were all men.

Both of the warriors carry spears in their hands and have swords latched to the back of their waistlines. One of them says, "The *Lakan* has sent us over to ensure that you will bring the *Babaylan* and her champion to his presence at once." Nadya's eyes become cold. Not cold, but hungry—eyes of a warrior, like the eyes of the women before us.

"I was on my way to retrieve *Ate Lanie* and the foreigners until I stumbled upon one of them already in the city. We got a little distracted," she shrugs.

I take a big gulp, feeling immense pressure from the tense energy.

Nadya looks over to me, "We must go now to *Lakan Ravi.* Time for you to meet my father."

We arrive in a large palace, the entire framing and structure made of large brown bamboo poles, a thatched roof covering the entire building. The palace is grander and much larger than the homes of the village. As we enter inside, I notice that even the floors are made of bamboo.

"Welcome to my home, the Bamboo Palace," says Nadya.

We enter a much larger room. It is an audience hall of royal magnificence. I see the audience hall finished in sandalwood. Large bamboo poles hold the structure in each corner.

Lakan Ravi sits in the middle of the hall, his bronze skin and tattoos unmistakably like Nadya's. He sits on a huge throne carved from bamboo and lined in gold and jewels. Like the sun, the *Lakan* shines brightly, the splendor of his court and presence evident in his magnificence. *Lakan Ravi* wears a jade green inner robe with long sleeves made of silk. Over the top of his inner robe is a golden-threaded fabric a well embroidered tunic, buttons made of jewels. On his head is a straw hat with a lining of dangled beads of emerald held by strings. Both of his ears hold massive golden-plated earrings. Golden beads and chains drape across his body like the citizens of *Jati*. Beside him sits another bamboo throne. Heavy plaques of gold line this throne, embroidered with jewels, as well.

Princess Nadya walks up the steps of the platform. She takes a bow before seating herself in the empty throne. One warrior follows her and stands next to her while the other warrior is stationed next to me, keeping an eye on my every move. The warriors bow, and I awkwardly do the same, before we sit in the hall's audience chairs.

Princess Nadya gestures her hand to speak, "Father, oh paramount ruler of the Kingdom of *Taal*, as instructed I have brought Salem, one of the foreigners here, to aid the champion of the prophecy."

Princess Nadya gives me a look and tilts her head upward, a signal to stand. Nervously, I rise from my seat and bow again, "Greetings, oh Great *Lakan Ravi*," I say.

"Welcome," he says. One simple word, yet it echoes throughout the room, reigning supreme, "Daughter, I remember I had requested the audience of both foreigners and the *Babaylan* Lanie."

Nadya crosses her arms and looks away, "I experienced an unexpected delay while finding the other," she says adamantly. I chuckled a little at her cunning response.

"And what was the delay?" he inquires.

Oh no, I think myself. *This is it.*

Before Nadya can answer, the doors of the hall open. I look back to see *Ate Lanie* and Mala walking in, "Worry, not *Lakan Ravi*, we have arrived. I am here with the champion of the prophecy, Mala of *Zambo*."

Saved again by Ate Lanie.

"*Ku ku ku* and it looks like their *Kuya* has arrived as well," she says.

The two join me and the warrior. They both bow and sit down. "I told you we would see you again soon," *Ate Lanie* whispers to me. *Must be her shaman powers, but her timing could have been better.*

"So it is true, the lunar legacy in the flesh amidst our kingdom," *Lakan Ravi* says, "But how can you confirm such an identity?"

Mala takes off their back pouch and pulls out the copperplate, "*Lakan Ravi*, inscribed on this copperplate are the details of the prophecy written in *Baybayin*. It was passed down from *Babaylan* to *Babaylan* for generations until I found it again back in my home, *Zambo*."

"Might I add, *Lakan*, on the shores before they arrived, Mala had created a great wall of water under the light of the Moon. The warriors who were there to save these two can attest to seeing it, as well. Only the lunar legacy, the shaman who draws power from the Moon, can control the tide at such great lengths," vouches *Ate Lanie*.

Some of the warriors in the hall nodded their heads to confirm.

"Very well. I trust *Babaylan* Lanie and the warriors of this court. The copperplate has returned to this island. With the upcoming lunar eclipse, we must act with haste," says *Lakan Ravi*.

"Unfortunately, the issue with the *Tikbalang* still remains," Nadya reminds, "Shall we start preparations for this trip?"

"Yes, the Keeper of the Forest of Lost Ones. The Enchanted Lake lies deep within the forest. We would need to have a plan to avoid falling victim to the *Tikbalang*'s disarray. *Babaylan*, what do you suggest?" asks the *Lakan*.

"Alone, I don't believe we could venture to the forest with even the bravest of warriors. But after today, I can see Mala's talent. With the two of us together, we should be able to fend off the Beast King. *Ku ku ku*, you see, the *Tikbalang* has a vulnerability," she says. "In order to subdue the beast, we must be able to pull one of its golden hairs. That is the only way to tame the *Tikbalang*."

That seems doable.

"Yes, but it has never been done before. The *Tikbalang* is twice as fast as a horse and glides through the shadows. We'd have to catch it first."

Never mind.

"I cannot send my warriors without reassurance that they will return," says the *Lakan*.

"No, we have no choice!" I blurt out. The room goes silent, everyone stares. "Uh-I mean…no, I mean exactly that. *Lakan Ravi*, I understand your sentiments, but the lunar eclipse is two nights after tonight. If we don't try…we will lose the Moon." I look over to see Nadya nodding in agreement. Then, I look over to Mala, who smiles back. *My Ading needs me. I can't accept a no, not even from a king.* "With or without the *Taal* warriors, I will accompany Mala and *Ate Lanie* through the Forrest of Lost Ones. I am a hunter from *Zambo*, I will hunt the Beast King if I must," I declare.

"Such bold words from a child," scolds the *Lakan*.

"But the young warrior is right. We do not have time. I will be joining the two in their quest," says *Ate Lanie*. *I am glad to hear her refer me as a warrior.*

"I can't leave my only *Babaylan* of the kingdom unprotected without some of my warriors."

"I will go, too!" shouts Nadya, standing triumphantly off her throne.

"No, Nadya. It's too dangerous a quest," says *Lakan Ravi*, "You have never dealt with the likes of the Beast King."

She removes her tiara and hands it to the warrior next to her, letting her long, black hair fall down past her shoulders. Her wild eyes light up and she jumps from the top platform firmly landing on her two feet on the ground level of the bamboo floors. She turns around to her father and, smirking, says, "Father, I am your greatest warrior. This quest needs me."

Warrior? She is a warrior, too. My heart thumps like the flopping of a great catch of fish.

"I would be honored to aid them in saving our people from the next Blood Moon. What princess warrior would I be to knowingly abandon them?" she asks.

"*Ku ku ku*, your daughter is an admired warrior. She takes after you, *Lakan*," smiles *Ate Lanie*.

"I believe it is settled then," Nadya says, putting her hands on her hips, her posture tall and sturdy in defiance of her father.

At first, *Lakan Ravi* says nothing. He is stern in his decision. But Nadya does not back down from her father. Then, he lets out a deep sigh, "Very well, then. But you must go with your entrusted warrior companions, Aysha and Nami." The two warriors from earlier bow their heads in response. "I cannot tame the wild spirit of my daughter. Even if I sent my warriors to keep you here, you would just defeat them in battle. When Nadya makes a decision, it is final. That is what I admire and respect about you, my daughter. I trust you. Please use your best judgment," he says solemnly.

"I suggest we head out in the morning. The *Tikbalang* is most active at night and in darkness. We can sneak through the forest during the day if we do not make too much noise. We can reach the Enchanted Lake before nightfall," says *Ate Lanie*.

"I agree. Tonight, we rest. At daybreak, we head for the Forest of Lost Ones," announces Nadya.

CHAPTER 8

FIGHT OR FLIGHT

Salem

Daybreak, and we set off on our mission through the Forest of Lost Ones. The trees that dominate the land are the largest I have ever seen, the leaves almost covering the soft purple and orange sunrise on the horizon. I wonder how a forest could become so whimsical in the presence of the *Tikbalang*. I am nervous about facing the creature. All I can remember is my encounter with the *Manananggal* and how I wasn't able to protect Mala. I feel weak. *Of course, this time around, we have warriors on our side.*

I turn around to get a glimpse of Nadya in her warrior attire. She is dressed like the women warriors, wearing red cloth, showcasing more of her bronze skin. I see that she has many more tribal tattoos lined all over her slim, athletic body. In one hand, she holds a *sibat*[29] made of long bamboo, its pointed edge carved with stone, and in the other hand she grips a circular, wooden *tameng*.[30] Behind her waist, she

---

29   Sibat – Spear
30   Tameng – Shield

carries another large sharp weapon, a *golok*,[31] and she has a *latigo*[32] coiled at her side. *She is indeed a talented warrior, equipped and prepared for battle in case of any ambush from any enemy that comes her way.*

"Are you okay, *Kuya*?" Mala asks.

I snap out of my thoughts, "Yes, *Ading*, I'm fine."

They smile and give me a gentle rub on my shoulder, "I could feel your aura had shifted. Don't worry, we will be okay." They walk ahead of me, their *bukaw* perched on their shoulder.

"I see you have become friends with the eagle owl."

"Yes, his name is *Kalma*. We've made an *abyan* pact to be friends. He is now my spirit companion."

I am glad for Mala. They are making friends—even if it is with a bukaw. I am glad they are finding some footing with their role as a Babaylan. They seem happier.

The uphill slope is tiring but it feels like the jungles of *Zambo*. I feel safer having the powerful warriors alongside me while venturing into these unknown forests. I have my trusted long bow *pana*, arrows, and my sword.

We walk quietly to avoid waking the Beast King from its daylight slumber, the ambiance of the woodland nature echoing around us. As we make our way through the forest, I notice marks on the ground. "Nadya, come look at this. These are huge hoof prints, dug several inches deep into the mud."

"These must be the *Tikbalang*'s prints! Let's keep moving, we are getting close to the Enchanted Lake. We are almost halfway through," she says.

---

31   Golok – Broadsword machete

32   Latigo – Long whip

I look over to Mala, who suddenly stops moving in their tracks. *Ate Lanie* does the same.

"What's wrong?" I ask them.

"Impossible," says Mala. "I feel a vibration of energy in the air in the woods."

"Is it a creature of the forest," says Nadya as she draws out her *golok blade* and prepares her *latigo* whip.

"No, it can't be. This energy feels human," Mala says.

"Yes, the force that drives them is close. They are coming," says *Ate Lanie* in an ominous tone.

Who is coming?

An arrow hits a nearby tree, barely missing me. "Watch out!" I yell, "It's the Blood Moon Knights!"

"Prepare for battle!" hollers Nadya.

We are ambushed. I can see three archers peak out from different sides of the forest. Three other men with their swords start rushing out of the trees. They wear padded chainmail that is cloaked all over their bodies. The seal of the serpent, crimson red, is branded on their metal chests. Metal helmets cover their faces.

Nadya fights off the two men, her spear striking one of the warriors. Her blade blocks another incoming attack. The two *Taal* warriors also fight. Aysha begins to battle one enemy, while I watch Nami run through the trees, dodging arrows, darting to the far archers.

I know Mala is defenseless without the Moon. They can't use their shaman powers. I have to protect them. I quickly look over to them and see one of the warriors coming at them.

"Arrrgh!" the man yells. *Kalma* spreads his large wings and glides fiercely at the warrior's face, causing a delay in his movement.

Thanks to the *bukaw*, I maneuver just in time to protect Mala. As I pull out my sword, the momentum of my swing parries the enemy attack, knocking the sword out of his hand. His helmet flies off from the impact.

"Are you okay?" I yell to Mala.

"Yes, *Kuya, Salamat!*"

I look over to the warrior on the ground and recognize the knight. *Tagyo! This must mean that the men I trained with have been initiated.*

"Protecting the monster of *Zambo*? You both are monsters that need to be slain," says Tagyo as he begins to get up.

My blood boils. *I can finally give him the beating he deserves.* I rush over and kick him back to the ground before he can stand. With the blunt handle of my blade, I strike him on the head and stun him. "Hmph, you could never be my brother-in-arms," I say. *But if he is here, that must mean...*

"Look out, *Kuya!*" warns Mala.

Another blade comes flying from behind my back. I try to dodge it, but my reaction is too slow as the edge of the sword slices the surface of my arm.

"Well, if it isn't our 'dear' hunter boy," says the Blood Moon Knight. *That voice, it can't be.*

"Sir Baskel!"

"It is so disappointing to see you here. You had so much potential to become a Blood Moon Knight. Now, here you are—a traitor to the Blood Moon cause."

"I'm not the traitor, Baskel. You've all been brainwashed by the *Bakunawa* to destroy the world. She's using you all as pawns!"

"Silence, you insolent renegade!" he yells, slashing his sword at me. I quickly evade it, moving backward just in time. "You must pay for your actions. Your blood must spill in the name of the Great Serpent."

Our blades dance in the air, clashing loudly together. He successfully evades each of my swipes. I could never beat him during our mock sword fights. Sir Baskel has years behind his skill with the sword. He has the upper hand. Baskel lunges his sword forward, pushing me to move backward to avoid the blade. I stumble and trip onto the floor. There, Baskel drives the blade down, ready to stab me into the ground. I quickly roll over, evading the blade by milliseconds. I kick Baskel in the knee, causing him to kneel. With this opening, I rush to the nearest tree.

"Archers, shoot him," Baskel commands.

I can't beat him in a sword fight, but I can't let him win. I am a hunter, and Baskel isn't. I have the agility of the predators that hunt their prey in the forests. The environment of the forest is my advantage. I have to trust my instincts.

While he tries to get up, I quickly climb the trunk of the nearest tree, dodging the arrows flying at me from all directions. I leap onto the closest branch and settle on top of it. Arrows continue to fly toward me. I quickly evade them by grabbing the branch with the grip of my calves. I hang upside down, facing Baskel. I pull out my arrow and I prepare my long bow *pana*. I take a deep breath and close in my eyes, gently grabbing the arrow and pulling it back in the bow. My hands and fingers relax—I have full control of the bow. I shoot a steady shot; the arrow darts through the wide-open space. It pierces through Baskel's hands, causing him to drop his sword. He stands, defenseless, and I backflip out of the tree, landing on my feet. I rush to tackle Baskel onto the ground. My body is heavy on top of him. I take off his helmet and see his agitated face. I bring out my sword, the edge of the blade touching his exposed neck.

"Do it," Baskel says, "finish me off."

I raise my blade in the air, ready to strike, but then stop. *I can't kill him. I'm no murderer.* I flip the blade to its hilt and swing it to Baskel's head, knocking him out.

Then, I hear a scream. I look over to see *Ate Lanie* yelling.

My eyes widen and my body trembles—the man holding her captive... is Father.

Nadya, Aysha, and Nami circle back from their fights, lowering their weapons. The warriors grasp them from behind. The archers all have their bows aimed at us. We are defenseless.

Father stands before me, clear as day, overbearing and pompous. He is the only Blood Moon Knight with armor draped in a red cape, indicating that he led the conquest from *Zambo*. Without his helmet, I see his mature and chiseled face, his long black hair flowing in the wind. His cold, dark eyes look right at me—his glare like the sharpness of his blade. "It brings me great sadness and embarrassment to have a traitor as my son," he says while he roughly clutches onto *Ate Lanie*, "What a great shame, Salem the betrayer."

Without hesitation, I get off Baskel and rush over to Father. "Arrrrgh!" I yell, swinging my blade at him. With only his right hand, he successfully parries my attack, knocking me back onto the ground. His laugh is exultant and powerful, "Still weak, poor child. You really think yourself a warrior!"

"Father? It can't be," says Mala.

"And here is the other disappointment—Mala the witch— the Monster of *Zambo*."

"What—what are you doing here?" asks Mala.

"When I found out my own children were the cause of this trouble, acting against the *Bakunawa*'s grand wishes, I took it upon myself to stop you. It is time you both suffer the consequences of the Blood Moon."

"How did you find us?" I manage to ask, slowly getting up.

"Don't you remember—the blessings of food gifted by the Keepers of the Temple of Serpents!" he says.

Blessings? Oh.

"The food that was gifted by the temple before the final ritual…I remember cooking it. We ate it the night we left," I say. *I did this. I brought them to us. I betrayed Mala.*

"Yes. Right before the initiation, the food you both ate was blessed by the *Bakunawa*. It tied her spirit to yours and led us right to you. Now, you will have no choice but to show us where the Mask of Gold rests, so that we can destroy it before the lunar eclipse," says Father.

Ate Lanie continues to struggle. "No! They can't find the mask! Don't worry about me!"

But how can she say that? I can't desert her. None of us can leave Ate Lanie.

"What a troublesome witch you are," Father says, pulling out a dagger from his belt. The dagger has two sharp edges, each shaped like serpents. The tails are the point of the blades and the body of each edge wraps over each other, meeting at the silver hilt of the dagger at the mouths of the two serpents. The blade is crimson red, like it is stained deep in blood. Then it hits me, it can only be the sacred Serpent's Dagger, stained by the blood of the many Blood Moon Knights who have cut their palms with it.

Father drives the dagger into the back of *Ate Lanie*'s shoulder, causing her to shriek. The scream radiates throughout the forest. I stare at her, helpless. She agonizes in pain as if the stabbing did more than hurt her body. The plants around her suddenly wither. I see a bright flashing light glow from the mark of her wound. Then, the light slowly wraps itself around the dagger. The light slowly fades and is absorbed. *Does the Serpent's Dagger have the power to take her magic?*

Right before she faints, Father throws her spiritless body to the ground. Quickly, I rush over to catch *Ate Lanie* as she falls. *She's still breathing. Thank the gods she is alive.* I take off my cloth head band and wrap it over her shoulder, tending to her wound.

"What did you just do?" Nadya spits in my father's direction.

"I took away her magic," he says with an evil grin. "I couldn't risk her using her sorcery. This is a scared blade blessed from the Temple of Serpents. Her spiritual essence is trapped in this blade and it now belongs to the *Bakunawa*."

I look over to Mala, their tears hitting the forest floor. *Kalma* had flown back to their shoulder trying to comfort them.

"Don't worry, my child, we still need your magic to retrieve the Mask of Gold, but you will be the *Bakunawa*'s soon enough," says Father.

I couldn't protect Mala. I couldn't even save Ate Lanie, who has saved me. The tears on my face began to drip down. *How can I be such a failure?*

Baskel gets up from the ground and grabs hold of me. Tagyo grabs Mala, "You're ours now to use, monster!" he shouts.

We start walking with the Blood Moon Knights, Baskel holding me hostage as I carry *Ate Lanie* in my arms. Nadya leads us through the forest at Father's imprisoning behest. An evening drizzle begins to fall as a shroud of dark clouds cover the sky.

As we continue to walk, I start to recognize the same trees and landmarks within the forest, like we are going in circles. The smell of smoke manifests and lingers.

"What is this trickery? You are leading us in circles," Father says threateningly, pointing his sword to Nadya's face.

"It's not me who is causing this! This doesn't bode well for us either," she responds.

"I feel the energy of a great spiritual aura coming," says Mala.

I feel a sudden gust of wind flow in the air. I hear the fierce rustle of the leaves of the trees followed by an eerie neigh ringing ominously through the forest. I glimpse a shadowy figure gliding above the trees.

The shadowy figure finally lands in front of us—half horse and half man. *The Beast King.*

CHAPTER 9

THE BEAST KING

Mala

The *Tikbalang* has the head of a great stallion, and the creature is as tall as our home back in *Zambo*. He has glaring eyes that pierce through my spirit. His upper body is that of a muscular man—its limbs are eerily long and extend all the way to the ground—his large, claw-like hands touching the dirt. His lower limbs are the hooves of a horse. The *Tikbalang* neighs and sounds almost like he is laughing, his golden mane flowing in the air. The stench of smoke reeks in his presence.

I lock eyes with the *Tikbalang*'s stare. I start to feel lost in his yellow, wild eyes. I feel his aura. The energy of the creature feels like the rumble of an earthquake. The pressure is even greater than that of the *Manananggal. So, this is the Beast King.* My head starts to hurt and the vibrations of the *Tikbalang* project loudly, ringing. I can't think straight as he clouds my head.

I look over and see the Blood Moon Knights let go of our group, preparing arms to battle the beast. Salem lays *Ate Lanie* by a nearby tree and prepares his bow and arrow.

Nadya and the warrior women ready their spears and blades. My eyes begin to water from the stench of the smoke. I cough and can see that the others are also affected. Salem struggles to find a clear shot of the beast.

Father commands his warriors to attack. The archers and knights' helmets must protect them from the smoke. The Blood Moon Knights shoot their arrows and ready their swords, aiming for the beast.

The *Tikbalang* lets out another roar-like neigh. The *Tikbalang*'s golden mane glows brightly like *Tala*'s stars in the night sky. The creature is fast, his horse-limbed hooves galloping with each stride, shaking the ground of the forest. He launches himself toward the archers, striking them. Nadya and Salem are swiped to the ground, caught in the blow.

The other men's strong confidence that once blazed like fire quickly dissipates into a feeling of sharp coldness, creating a tightness in my chest. Anxiety fills the air as the commotion from the Beast King worsens. My head is dizzy, and I start to lose control of my own senses. Many of the warriors begin to tremble and run into the forest. I feel the warrior holding me shake, as well, frozen in his tracks.

"Cowards!" yells Father. He looks over to me and commands the knight to bring me to him.

No way!

I kick the knight, escaping his grasp and run toward Salem. I look up and see the *Tikbalang*'s golden mane and large shadowy physique above me. My eyes widen before his immense presence. The *lakas* of the Beast King towered, my mind lost in his flow of energy. The *Tikbalang* looks down on me, his yellow glaring eyes staring again. It feels like chaos. My mind is blank, and my heart is racing. The shortness of my breath makes the tightness of my chest hurt more. *Is this what pure fear feels like? I didn't feel this way with the Manananggal.*

A blast of air rushes past my face as, the *Tikbalang* disappears into the trees, chasing after the knights and Father, who had all run into the forest. His high-pitched sound echoes in my ears as if he never left. I pet *Kalma*'s head to comfort him, but I notice he is unaffected by the *Tikbalang*'s presence. I look over to check on the rest of the group, everyone dusting themselves off from the sudden attack. Their auras are filled with coldness, their anxiety clear. We all take a moment to collect ourselves.

"Well, looks like our plan to sneak past the Beast King is over," says Salem.

"It must have woken up from its slumber from the noise of our battle," says Nadya.

Ate Lanie begins to wake up. I could sense her aura, as well, unaffected by the *Tikbalang*. Her vibrations are normal, and her spirit feels warm like always, but the absence of her special *lakas* power is concerning. I wonder if she will ever fully recover from the attack. We all huddle toward her.

"*Ate Lanie*, are you okay?" I ask.

"*Ku ku ku*," she manages to laugh, "I am alive." She tries to get up but flinches from the pain of her wound.

"Here, let us help you," Salem says. We both help her to stand.

I cannot fathom Father's wickedness. *How he could hurt Ate Lanie like this?* The thought makes my stomach hurt. "We're so sorry our father did this to you," I say.

"We're going to make him pay," says Salem.

"Worry not, my dear children. It is not your responsibility to bear the burden of your father's action. We must only move forward from here. We have no time."

Ate Lanie is right. The only way to right this wrong is to find the Mask of Gold before he and the Bakunawa do.

"Where are the Blood Moon Knights?" she asks.

"They fled into the forest, running away once the *Tikbalang* showed up," says Nadya.

"The Beast King...he is awake. He must have chased after them to play with their fears. But he will be back for us, too," *Ate Lanie* confirms.

"How can we prepare to fight him?" I ask.

"He wants to drive us mad. The longer we stay in the forest, the madder we become. He is a creature that finds our lunacy amusing. The *Tikbalang* plays with our minds for pleasure. He will continue to feed on our madness to gain energy and power over us," says *Ate Lanie*.

"Well, how can we leave the forest? We have been traveling in circles!" says Nadya.

"At its worst, the Beast King has only been known to lead people astray and play mischievous tricks on their senses. The madness affects you worse when you stare it right in its wild yellow eyes." *Oh no. I stared right at them.* I shudder and remember how staring at the *Tikbalang's* eyes felt like my soul had been pierced. "He's a gatekeeper, not a killer. He protects this realm of the forest. We can only leave if he wants us to leave. Once we subdue the Beast King, we can continue toward the Enchanted Lake," explains *Ate Lanie*.

"So, let me be clear. What you're saying is that we'll need to wrestle that creature and steal a piece of its mane in order to control it?" says Salem.

"Exactly," says *Ate Lanie*.

"You're just as mad as the creature," he says.

"*Ku ku ku.* You have another idea?"

"You're right. We'll need a plan. Should we keep walking?" I ask.

"We will be walking without direction. It's best if we stay here and stay close. We can learn from the Blood Moon Knights and try to ambush it," suggests Salem.

"Brilliant idea, Salem!" says Nadya.

Dusk began to settle in the forest and the darkness of the night shrouded the area, adding to the layer of anxiety in my mind. I can't help but feel that I am being watched. My spine begins to tingle. The tingle, like spiders, crawls throughout my entire body, causing me to shiver uncontrollably. The darkness of the night begins to feel cold and tastes strangely bitter, like smoke.

This unusual feeling begins to grow stronger. The darkness feels colder, and I can't stop imagining the yellow glare of the *Tikbalang*'s eyes as I move in the darkness. These bright yellow eyes of madness follow me everywhere I go. First, the one pair one eyes appeared. *I must be seeing things.* I rub my eyes, and as I open them again, I now see two pairs of eyes. With another blink, I see dozens of yellow eyes appear all around me. "AAHHH!" I scream.

"What's wrong, Mala?" Salem asks. But when I look at him, he has the head of a stallion. *It's not real,* I keep repeating to myself. I can only see the eyes of the *Tikbalang* around me. I start to hyperventilate.

The ringing in my ears grows louder until the sound of the ring transforms into robust *neighs.* I crouch down and cover my ears. The coldness of the air starts to suffocate me. Out of nowhere, strong hands grab me by the shoulders. *It is the Tikbalang!* I shake off their claws.

I look up and realize they are *Ate Lanie*'s hands, "Mala, did you stare into the eyes of the *Tikbalang*?"

I nod slowly, "It was an accident."

"You need to strengthen your mind. The Beast King is playing tricks on you and heightening your perception of reality. You need to breathe slowly and remember it's not real. Relax and let the energy of your *abyan*'s spirit calm you. Remember, you have *Kalma*."

Yes, she is right. The fear is not real. I need to draw energy from my abyan. That must be why Kalma wasn't affected, his calming nature is so strong that even the Tikbalang can't penetrate his generations of wisdom.

I take a deep breath and stare into *Kalma*'s eyes. I listen to the sounds of the beautiful and simple chimes that feed into my ears and recall the feeling of clarity. My mind clears and I acknowledge the pain points in my mind. Even with *Kalma*'s help, the power of the *Tikbalang*'s aura was still there, deep inside as if he had planted a deep seed of his *lakas*—a parasite stuck in my head. My resolve needs to be stronger. This is a test of wills. I begin to understand the *Tikbalang*'s mind games.

"*Salamat, Abyan*," I say as I rub *Kalma*'s back. He coos contently.

I realize that his magic power is feeding off my fear and insecurities, manifesting them into reality. *Its domain is this forest. The forest is real. The madness is not. After being inside the mind of the Tikbalang, maybe the answer is not to get out of his head. Does the Beast King want me in his head? Is he trying to show me something?*

"I have an idea, but it's a little mad," I say, "The *Tikbalang* thinks I'm afraid of it. After staring at its eyes, I am the target of its lunacy. I can turn my weakness to our advantage—use me as bait."

Whenever I am afraid, I hold onto the pearls of my mother's necklace. It helps me to not feel alone in my moments of fear. Fear of the dark, fear of the unknown, fear of losing myself— all the fears in the world, and I hide away at the thought of my mother's spirit protecting me.

But this time, I know this won't work. As bait, I need to let the Beast King feel like he is winning. It is time I face my fears head on and lose my mind completely to the *Tikbalang*. I hold onto mother's pearl necklace, not as a shield against fear, but as a reminder that I will get through this.

The night feels long and never-ending, as I sit down in silence, waiting for the *Tikbalang* to arrive and finish what he started. The drizzling rain continues to fall from the dark clouded sky, and I am alone in the darkness. The Moon shines brightly, and I can see its slight glimmer behind the darkness of the clouds, but because it is the last night before the Blood Moon, I remember the imminent danger lying ahead. *The lunar eclipse is tomorrow night. We only have one chance at success left.* Thinking of the *Bakunawa* triggers a deep fear within me. The people of *Taal*, *Zambo*, and the islands will suffer great imbalance and chaos if I fail. I slowly feel my mind lose itself to the madness as my own thoughts and worries torment me.

Eventually, I feel the rumble of vibrations. The *Tikbalang* quakes the forest floor with the heavy stomps of his hooves. A deep stench of smoke comes closer and closer until its presence surrounds me. I close my eyes and absorb the pressure of the powerful spirit approaching. The *Tikbalang* is now in front of me and lets out a robust *neigh*, rumbling the ground of the Earth.

I feel the madness creeping in, this time growing stronger. It is harder to control my aura, the beast paints worrisome hallucinations in my mind. *They're not real,* I try to ground myself. I imagine Salem being burned alive—then Nadya, *Ate Lanie, Kalma* and the warriors all engulfed in flames. The smell of smoke makes it feel all too real. Even in the drizzling rain, the visions of my loved ones in fire won't stop. I feel tears in my eyes, my body shaking completely as I am helpless to save my loved ones. *Is this the reality of which I am truly afraid? That I will fail to protect my home and loved ones?* Then it occurs to me—this feeling of fear is how the *Tikbalang* is feeling, too. His fears are being manifested through my mind.

I take a deep breath and open my eyes, staring directly at the *Tikbalang*. I allow his energy to enter through me, the way I did with *Kalma*. I start to feel his *lakas* flow through me. This time I am not lost in his madness. I am a part of it, our minds and souls connected. I begin to understand why he wants me to feel pain from my fear. He must have chosen to communicate with me because I am a *Babaylan*. I am the only one who has the power to feel his *lakas* energy. I can understand his emotions.

The Beast King feels trapped—the madness is a result of the pain he feels for the humans who have invaded his home and hurt the creatures and their land. He is fearful of the disturbance of the coming Blood Moon. He remembers what happened years ago, how the *Bakunawa* terrorized his lands before. I realize the *Tikbalang* is afraid, too, of failing to protect his forest and the creatures who live in his domain.

"You're not a monster either, are you, Beast King? You're just trying to protect your home. We can help you," I say, staring in his yellow eyes, but no longer feeling fear or lost in his madness.

At first the *Tikbalang* is reluctant, but then he approaches me. He lets out a soft neigh. As I reach out to touch him, I suddenly feel the shift in his nature. He is still too distrustful and fearful of humans and lets out a magnificent roar. He raises his claw and, as the beast is about to strike me down, Salem's arrow shoots from a nearby tree. The arrow startles the *Tikbalang* causing him to dodge left.

As the *Tikbalang* lunges its body to evade the arrow, Nadya leaps off the branches of the tree and onto the *Tikbalang*. She comes flying downward, landing on top of him and grabbing hold of his back. With one hand, she grabs her *latigo* whip and strikes the *Tikbalang* on the back of his legs, causing the beast to wail in pain and get on all fours.

She wraps her whip like a lasso around his neck, tying it like a rope and securing her position on the back of the beast. He begins to wildly fly from tree to tree, attempting to push off Nadya from his rein. But the princess is strong, even stronger in will. Her exuberant yells echo throughout the forest with the uproarious neighs of the *Tikbalang*, both struggling in their wrestling match. With a grasp of her hand, she rips out a handful of the *Tikbalang*'s golden mane, imposing her power and subduing the beast. The Beast King lets out a shrieking neigh that pulses through the trees, then he finally relaxes on the ground.

The drizzling rain begins to fade away. I see rays of the light beaming through as the dark clouds covering the entire forest begin to dissipate, revealing the clear daylight of the sky. *It looks like the night had ended a while ago. The*

Tikbalang must have created those clouds to hide the day-light. It is a magnificent view, seeing Nadya, fist full of golden hair raised high in the sky. She belts out a victory cry, and Aysha and Nami join her as they come out of the bushes.

Salem comes down from his tree, both his fists in the air, "By the gods, we actually did it! We tamed the Beast King!"

Yes, we did. Together.

Like a great stallion, the *Tikbalang* stands proud, bowing his head at me. I approach the beast slowly and look at its eyes, no longer glaring yellow with madness. Instead, they are a beautiful green, reminding me of the foliage of the forest. Inside the lens of the eyes are golden rings, reflecting its mane. I reach over and pet the top of his head. My forehead touches his and I feel a calming aura, no longer like tsunamis but more like the shallow ripples of waves. The ringing is no longer there. "You no longer need to be afraid, our new friend. You can trust us," I tell him, relieved.

Nadya lends down her hand, and I grab hold of it. She pulls me up to mount the beast with her, "We can all fit on top of the back of the *Tikbalang*," she says.

Salem and the warriors help carry *Ate Lanie* to the back of the beast and we all grab his mane. *Kalma* perches himself back onto my shoulder.

Nadya gently rubs the mane. She asks him, "What shall I name you, our new friend of the forest?"

"How about pain in the neck?" shouts Salem.

Nadya giggles, "Don't disrespect him!" She pauses, stroking the Beast King's glorious mane. "It's like I said last time. I have always wanted to bring peace between our tribes and with the Beast King."

Nadya takes a brief moment to think, then she announces triumphantly, "I shall name thee, *Ulap!*"

"Cloud?" asks Salem.

"Yes, *Ulap* as in 'cloud.' You see, a cloud comes from anything burning. *Ulap* gives off the smell of smoke while also summoning very light rain. He's a cloud of many things."

"I see it. I like that, too. It's perfect, Nadya," I say.

"We must make haste. With the *Tikbalang* subdued, the madness that causes people to be lost in the forest has now stopped. The Blood Moon Knights still linger in these lands," warns *Ate Lanie*.

"But we will get to the Enchanted Lake much faster than they will now with the help of *Ulap*. Our dear Beast King, lead us out of your domain and toward the Enchanted Lake," says Nadya.

With this command, the *Tikbalang* obeys and, like a bolt of lightning, he speeds through the forest, jumping from tree to tree, gliding as if flying. The breeze feels amazing as Nadya leads the creature. It is as if she had ridden the creature before; a natural rider—Tamer of the Beast King. We are finally out of the woods.

CHAPTER 10

SISTERS OF THE
ISLA SIRENA

———

Mala

We finally depart from the Forest of Lost Ones. With each step forward, *Ulap* makes small rumbles, shaking the ground as he steadies toward the lake. As we grow close to the Enchanted Lake, I feel the powerful *lakas* from afar. It is calling me—like the time in the *Aklatan* when I first felt the call from the copperplate inscription.

Finally, we have arrived. Before I jump off, *Ate Lanie* stops me. "Take off your *bakyas*.[33] We are on sacred ground." I remove my wooden clogs and slide off *Ulap*'s forearm. Landing on the ground, my feet feel the soft, moist grass. My toes begin to curl and clench the soil. I take a deep breath to sense the purity of the air. I walk closer toward the lake, feeling the spiritual energy circulate around me. Each step feels like I am embracing the grass and the earth; I can't help

———

33   Bakyas – Wooden clogs; Traditional footwear

but feel that I have walked these lands before. The presence of the *lakas* from the lake is familiar, but I can't fully understand the memory.

"I can see why they call this the Enchanted Lake," I say.

"Really? Seems regular to me," Salem says as he counts the arrows left in his quiver.

"This is no regular lake; it is a spiritual basin with a grandiose supply of *lakas*. The amount of *lakas* that is generated from these waters flows throughout the entire island," says *Ate Lanie.*

"Yes, our people have relied on the source of *lakas* from the Enchanted Lake for many years, but since it is found in the middle of the Forest of Lost Ones, the Beast King has protected it from intruders," Nadya states, petting *Ulap*'s head. I sense *Ulap*'s quiet, calm vibrations and realize that *Ulap* trusts us on this sacred land.

I walk closer to the large lake. From a distance, I see that the lake encompasses the surrounding area of land. The sapphire waters shimmer beautifully in the sunlight. I feel the calm and tranquil serenity of the lake's presence. The vibrations of the energy are unlike anything I have felt before, emitting *lakas* energy and purifying my spirit, cleansing it of all negativity, stress, and fears. All the things that haunted me feel like they no longer exist. *Is this the enchanting power of the lake?*

"It has been years since I have been here. I have prayed in this place once before seeking refuge in this sanctuary," *Ate Lanie* sighs, approaching me. "Shall we make our way to the lake's shrine?" She points at a sanctified altar with a large arched gate at the edge of the lake. I see purple flowers lined around the entrance. As I get closer, I feel a gravitational pull. I see them, clear as day: the *Takay Flowers.*

I rush to the arched gate, its marble stone visibly strong. The *Takay Flowers* grow like flowering vines, almost covering the entire entrance, lunar energy emanating from their petals. *No silver glow this time though.*

Through the gate toward the edge of the lake is another marble pedestal with a deep indent. The shores are paraded with *Takay Flowers* that seem to only grow within the area of the shrine. In the distance I see a grand waterfall, directly in front of the shrine. The sounds of the roaring cascades are crisp in my ears. As I walk to the edge of the water, I feel a strong mystical allure, as if the water is calling for me to join and dip into it. My temptations get the best of me and I touch the water, instantly absorbed by its purifying properties. With just the touch of my hands in the lake's water, the sacred *lakas* flow within me. The overwhelming urge to bathe and swim within the lake and become entirely engulfed in its cool, fresh waters floods my mind. These waters feel safe, like I can escape my worries by cleansing myself here. I feel a sense of familiarity again. The physical touch of the water reminds me that I have been here before. The *lakas* energy does not feel new.

"This place, it feels like a distant memory," I say, looking back at *Ate Lanie*, "but I have never been here before."

"*Ku ku ku* this is the Shrine of Seven Moons! You must be connecting with the deep lunar roots of this place."

"Yes that makes sense. This shrine is connected deeply to the Moon. The *Takay Flowers* from my dream prove it. How are they growing here?"

"Well, legend has it that when the seven Moon siblings first graced this earth, the Enchanted Lake was the basin in which they bathed."

"I can understand why they bathed in these waters. The *lakas* that flow through it feel re-energizing. *Ate*

Lanie, if you bathed in these waters, would you regain your *lakas* power?"

"The sacred waters of the Enchanted Lake have purifying properties, but they do not have the power to grant me back my *lakas* of creation. This specific and special *lakas* power will require a different type of healing. But do not worry about me, Mala, for now we must focus on the Blood Moon first," she assures.

But how can I not worry about her? I want to help her as she has helped us. She is focused on the quest, and I need to be focused, too. There will be no way to help her if the Moon is gone.

"*Bulan*, the last Moon, spent most of his time here in this spot…Do you know of the story of how the *Takay Flowers* were first created?" asks *Ate Lanie*.

I shake my head.

Ate Lanie gestures with her hand, inviting me to relax on the ground, I sit with my feet crossed, the lavender flowers brushing against my skin.

"Well, my dear, legend has it that during one of the full Moons, *Bulan* descended to bathe in the waters of the Enchanted Lake. When he finished bathing, he came here, to his favorite spot on the shore, to lie in the green grass under the glow of the full Moon. While lying in the night, he heard a struggle in the water. From afar he could see a maiden that looked to be swimming alone in the lake. Then, he realized she was drowning in the waters. *Bulan* quickly swam through the lake to rescue her."

"Did he save her?"

"Sadly, by the time he had reached her body, it was already too late. He brought her body back to the shores of this shrine.

Bulan grieved—how the death of a human pained him so— and he met *Sidapa* during his cries in the night."

"His lover!"

"Yes, but not at the time. This was the beginning of their love story. *Sidapa* was so moved by *Bulan*'s empathy over the human's death, he offered to reincarnate her spirit rather than bring her soul to the Underworld."

"Reincarnate?"

Ate Lanie nods slowly, "That's right. Together with Sidapa, *Bulan* and the Deity of Death decided to use their powers and transform the maiden into a beautiful purple flower—purple reflecting the amethyst color of *Bulan*'s tears. This was the first ever water hyacinth to grow on this Earth."

"So the maiden was reborn into a *Takay Flower*. It seems like the tears of the Moon deities have powerful *lakas* that can even reincarnate the dead."

"Rule breakers, those lunar siblings are! *Ku ku ku*! The Moon represents rebirth. This is the root of the lunar power. These *Takay Flowers* represent this moment in our ancestral history, to remind us that, even in death, there is the beauty of transformation; a birth of something new. This is the bridge that connects the cycle of death and rebirth. Remember, *lakas* has the power to be transformed. With the right power, a lifeforce can be reborn anew."

The birth of something new. A symbol of my relationship with the Moon. Maybe that's what the Mask of Gold represents, too. "I see, *Ate Lanie*, it's the importance of balance between life and death."

"*Ku ku ku* our champion gets it!" She laughs. "During my prayers here, I would sometimes see *Sidapa* visiting this spot, staring at the moonlight as he gathered around himself the *Takay Flowers*."

Sidapa is so kind. "We will reunite them," I say. *I promised Sidapa that I would fulfill this quest. I can't let him down. I can't let anyone down. This is my history, too.*

"Although *Bulan* has not visited the Earth in a long time, his favorite spot still remains here, in the Shrine of Seven Moons, as a place to remember our loved ones who have passed away," says *Ate Lanie.*

I touch my pearl necklace again and think of my mother. "Could I take a moment to pray and remember my mother?"

Ate Lanie nods, "Take all the time you need."

I close my eyes.

Mother, I never got the chance to meet you, but I just want to thank you for all this time, your spirit watches over us.

I let the tranquil aura resonate within me and feel the spirit waves of the *Takay Flowers* flow within my body. It feels like my dream, when I was surrounded by the field of flowers in an endless garden. After a moment, I continue to pray to her.

I wish you were here. I rub the pearls on my neck and let myself feel the sorrow of not growing up with a mother; how lonely this felt. *Although I am not alone all the time, Mother. I have Salem, always here to watch over me. I grew up with someone I could trust. When the world rejected me, we had each other. You gave us the family we needed. You will always be in our hearts.*

I open my eyes. I felt good. I always speak to her in my thoughts, but this time it felt like my words really reached her—maybe because of the shrine.

I take a good look at the ivory pedestal—it is brilliant, carved in the finest marble and standing just as tall as I am. I walk over to examine it a bit more. The indent in the middle of the pedestal is peculiar, its shape was that of an asymmetrical puzzle piece. I immediately know where I have seen this shape before. I take the copperplate inscription out of my pouch, its outer shape mirroring the indent. I place the copperplate into the pedestal. *Perfect fit.*

A shining ray of light glows from the copperplate, radiating an immense *lakas* wave that bursts from the pedestal. The lake began to ripple boldly.

The ripples of the waves finally stop, but I feel a small series of waves from afar. *Is it coming from inside the lake?* As I focus my attention on the lake, I sense a unique energy, somewhat divine like when I was around *Sidapa*. Not one, but three life forces, their heavenly auras growing more and more as they approach. I get ready to defend my ground not sure what to expect, when suddenly a beautiful creature emerges from the water, her skin jade green. She looks to be a woman above her waistline, her skin glowing a light blue tattoo-like pattern, but her waist I recognize a serpent-tail, layered in emerald scales. Two matching beings, their skin tones are the color of their tails, emerge from the lake following after. They are tall and large, nearly the size of *Ulap*. The three divine beings slither their way onto the shores of the shrine in front of me.

Each water spirit has a distinct pattern of the scales of their tails. The first one's emerald scales were shaped liked jagged knives, the tips pointed, "We were summoned from the depths of the Enchanted Lake by the energy of the sacred copperplate. I am Hydrophis," she says.

The second has green, golden and red scales, with a seashell pattern, "I am Samar," she utters in a soft and charming tone.

The third has scales of copper with auburn hues, the scales rounded like rough, miniature shields, "I am Oligodon," she grunts heavily, the most headstrong of the three beings, "We are the *Naga* Sisters of *Isla Sirena*."

"It has been a long time since we have seen the likes of mortals arrive in the Enchanted Lake," reminisces Hydrophis.

"Yes, not since the *Tikbalang*, Guardian of the Forest has protected our sacred lake from humans," says Samar, "But the *lakas* of this child reminds me so much of the seven Moon siblings. What is your name?"

"I am Mala of *Zambo*, the lunar legacy and champion of the prophecy," I proudly announce.

"The lunar legacy has *finally* graced our presence? And on the night of the Blood Moon," criticizes Oligodon, in a tone of annoyance.

"You must be the *Nagas* that *Sidapa* mentioned. He said you are to help me on my quest," I tell them.

"We help no one but the secrets of the dead," responds Oligodon.

"What my sister means is that we are *Nagas*, guardians of water and wealth. It is our duty to protect the treasures deep within the earth. We do not answer to *Sidapa*," explains Hydrophis.

"But isn't *Sidapa* the king of the Underworld? Isn't he your *Lakan*?" I ask.

"*Sidapa* is the Deity of Death, yes. He rules the Underworld and the proceedings of a spirit's afterlife, mortal or supernatural," says Samar. "He rules the dead. We, on the other hand, were born and reside in the Underworld."

"We are of equal splendor and power to the Deity of Death. That realm is not his to rule on his own," announces Oligodon mightily.

"A spirit can journey itself into many kinds of afterlife. Our duty as *Nagas* is to guard their sacred wishes once they have passed. That is the treasure and wealth that we protect," Samar clarifies.

"As lunar legacy of the copperplate, you must be the heir to the Golden Moon," affirms Hydrophis.

"Golden Moon?" I ask.

"Yes, *Haliya*, one of the seven Moon siblings. Her eyes radiated golden like stars. Her mask treasure is hidden deep within the depths of the Enchanted Lake. Not even our sister *Bakunawa* can access it. The Goddess *Haliya*, who forged the Golden Mask from her tears for her fallen siblings, was brave enough to challenge our sister, *Bakunawa*. *Haliya*'s Golden Mask is now locked away, awaiting its rightful creator to return," responds Hydrophis.

"Both deities' resolve for revenge caused a great imbalance in our world. Lasting effects will take place if our sister successfully devours the last Moon in tonight's total lunar eclipse," warns Samar.

"We have protected this mask since the Battle of the Great Moons in hopes that a reincarnation of *Haliya* will return to finish the Great Battle against *Bakunawa*," says Oligodon.

The lunar legacy—the champion who is to complete the prophecy and procure the Mask of Gold to finish the Great Battle of Moons—is the reincarnation of Haliya! The Lunar Deity who actually fought Bakunawa and greatly injured the Deity of Eclipses. Could it really be me? Is that even possible?

"R-reincarnation? You can't mean me?" I stammer.

"Why, of course we mean you! How else could you be chosen as the lunar legacy to complete the prophecy?" answers Oligodon.

It all starts to make sense. My connection to the Moon. *Is this why I was chosen to go on this quest? Is my ability to feel the energy around me all because of Haliya?*

As I look back, I see that *Ate Lanie* has returned with Salem, *Ulap*, *Kalma*, Nadya, and her warrior companions. "Warriors halt your hostility. These are the Sacred *Naga* Sisters of our island. We must pay our respect to their home," she warns the group.

Ate Lanie, Nadya and her warriors bow to show respect. Salem follows shortly after.

"Well, I see you did not come on this quest alone this lifetime around," says Hydrophis.

"No, I couldn't have done it alone," I say.

"The night is coming, we must hurry and take you down to the depths of the water. *Bakunawa* will feel strongest at the time of the Blood Moon. This is when she will cast her eclipse and turn into the great serpent dragon once more," warns Samer.

"Only you can unlock the secrets to *Haliya*'s treasure," declares Hydrophis, her long sharp emerald nail pointing toward the Enchanted Lake.

"But what about the others," I gesture to my found family behind me, "I couldn't have gotten this far without them."

Salem comes up toward me and gives me a rub to my head with his fist, this time a lot rougher than usual. "We'll be fine, *Ading*. If the water spirits say you must do this alone, you must find the strength in yourself to do so."

He's right, I trust him. I trust all of them. We can do this. Together.

"You are not alone," says Nadya, "We'll protect you."

"We have got your back. Through thick and thin," says Salem.

Ulap lets out a loud neigh. The warriors Aysha and Nami also bow in solidarity. *Kalma* circles around the air and lands back on my shoulder.

"Our sister, *Bakunawa*, will be at her most vulnerable in her *Naga* form like us. She will not reach her strongest dragon form until the total lunar eclipse. She will try to come down into the Enchanted Lake to retrieve the Mask of Gold and destroy it before the lunar legacy gets a hold of it. You all must fend her off before this," says Oligodon.

This is it. Time to retrieve the Golden Mask and finish the quest. "But I can't swim deep into the depths of the lake. I can't possibly hold my breath for that long!"

Ate Lanie gets up from the ground and places her hand in the sky, "*Ku Ku Ku* remember our first meeting my dear?"

"Yes, we were in our astral projection state," I recall.

"Not only can your spirit fly upwards to reach the skies, but it can descend downwards as well, to the bottoms of the Earth."

"But I've never done it alone before!"

"This is not the first time you have projected yourself. Your mind is a powerful force. The trick is to let your consciousness flow with the projection of your *lakas* energy."

"In other words, be free, Mala," says Salem.

Free. I have always felt trapped in this body, but now I can flow—flow like the water that I have always known before—my newfound power.

"Your astral spirit is tethered to your physical body. As long as your physical body is safe, your soul can wander the likes of this realm fairly safely. Now, imagine what that freedom looks like to you, my dear," says *Ate Lanie*, "and let your mind take over from there."

I close my eyes and let the *lakas* energy flow like a river through my body and back out into the Enchanted Lake. I concentrate my consciousness and imagine a butterfly bursting out of a cocoon, fluttering its wings, finally free. And like the butterfly, I spread my wings too, breaking free my consciousness, into an astral projection. The *Nagas* see my essence and submerge themselves into the Enchanted Lake. I descend into the depths after them.

CHAPTER 11

NIGHT OF BLOOD MOON

——————

Salem

Mala's body is unmoving in their "astral state" as *Ate Lanie* explains to me. I am worried for Mala, but I need to trust them. I can't fail to protect them anymore. *This is it.* I look over to see Nadya ready her stead atop *Ulap*, her *latigo* whip and *sibat* spear ready for battle. Aysha and Nami prepare their weapons, as well. This time, I see them dipping their blades into an extract. Nami approaches me with the liquid and says, "Here, dip your bow and blade in this."

"What is it?" I ask.

"It's a paralyzing agent. The main ingredient is toxins produced by cassava root extract," says *Ate Lanie*, "I made it myself."

"Well this could've been useful earlier," I grumble.

"*Ku ku ku*, the cassava root is not naturally grown on our island. Because of our limited supply, we were saving all of it for our battle against the *Bakunawa*. We did not expect an ambush from the Blood Moon Knights in the forest, my dear."

Fair point. I take out my arrows and sword. I dip my weapons into the mixture. I look at my sword and recall the moment I almost slayed Baskel, and how I failed. *I'm not a killer like them.*

"The agent will only work once it has been exposed to torn flesh, so make sure to create an open wound for the solution to work," says *Ate Lanie.*

"It will be a great asset to us as we fight these knights. We need them alive to capture and interrogate them once this is all over," says Aysha.

The sun begins to set, the Blood Moon is coming, and so is the Deity of Eclipses.

All is silent.

"AAEERRCHHHHHHH!"

A loud screech blasts through the air. It is the *Manananggal! What is this beast doing here? It must have survived from the wave crash during our first encounter in the ocean.* The bat demon continues to soar the skies, its glaring red eyes as terrifying as the first time I saw them. But something is different: I notice a glowing red mark on the side of its upper torso.

The *Manananggal* lashes out its whip-like tongue at me. *Ulap* dashes in front of me and Nadya counters the tongue with her own *latigo* whip. The blow of their lashes strikes each other in the air, creating a loud snapping sound like lightning. Nadya throws her bamboo spear at the flying creature, but it evades it easily. I shoot an arrow, but the demon is too fast and avoids our every attack. The winged creature continues to screech in the skies, and *Ulap* belts out a loud neigh in an attempt to overcome the creature.

"Can't the Beast King control the *Manananggal*?" I yell.

"I'm not sure why the demon isn't being subservient to *Ulap*'s command. Something isn't right," Nadya yells back. *Nothing is ever right.*

From afar, I see the Blood Moon Knights coming, torches lit in their hands as they approach exiting the Forest of Lost Ones. Father is in front of the group, the Serpent's Dagger in his hand. *The dagger! Father must have stabbed the creature. Does it have properties to control it? If that is the case, then...*

I look over to see *Ate Lanie* lost in a trance, her hands ready to grasp Mala's physical body. *Sorry Ate Lanie,* I think as I tackle her body onto the shore. Her eyes look empty, but I can tell she is under Father's control.

"It's the Serpent's Dagger. It's controlling *Ate Lanie* and the *Manananggal*. I need rope!" I yell. Nadya throws a rope to *Kalma*, who flies above me and drops it to me. I tie *Ate Lanie's* wrists to her ankles, leaving her immobile. *Kalma* flies and circles *Ate Lanie*, guarding her body. I unwrap the cloth from her back and I see it too. The mark of the dagger, her scar glowing red. I clench my fists in rage. *So many lines have been crossed.* But I remember *Ate Lanie's* words. *I can't let anger take over my body.* I take a deep breath to think clearly. I need a new strategy to win this battle.

While *Ulap* and Nadya battle the demon bat, I exit the shrine gates with the *Taal* Warriors. We charge toward Father and his Blood Moon Knights.

I rush over to Father. Before I can reach him, Tagyo appears in front of me, followed by Sir Baskel. Their swords are armed and ready. "Two against one? Doesn't seem fair for a rematch. How dishonorable of you so-called knights," I say. I see anger in Tagyo's face, his ego so fragile that simple insults agitate him. As Tagyo screams, his sword ready to slash me, I notice an opportunity and sideswipe him from his feet, knocking him over.

Baskel follows right behind, piercing his sword straight forward toward me. "You insolent traitor!" he yells.

"The only traitor is you, Baskel! The Blood Moon Knights are a sham!" I yell back.

This provokes him and he yells toward me, ready to stab me with his sword. I see his movements clearly; they become easier to predict. He hasn't changed at all since our sparring. As the tip of the sword reaches me, I flex and execute a back-flip dodge. Baskel doesn't give up and he comes back at me with his sword. Another knight is in my peripheral sight. I breathe and listen to his steps. I calculate the timing, and dodge. Baskel strikes the other knight down as he tries to hit me.

I don't let anger and frustration hinder me in battle any longer. This time, I use these emotions against my opponents.

While Baskel is distracted, I pull out my *pana*. At first, I aim it at Baskel, but I realize Tagyo is rushing toward me. I draw back my arrow and shoot it at Tagyo's chainmail. I know my arrow heads are sharp enough to pierce through the chainmail and reach skin. The arrow strikes Tagyo's leg; he immediately falls on the floor, paralyzed.

"I can't move!" he yells out.

"Careful men, their weapons have been bewitched!" warns Baskel.

The Blood Moon Knights are reluctant to attack this time, but the men circle around me with their swords. I take a step forward, and the men step back. Their reluctance is my advantage. I have more space to think clearly for my next move. I prepare my *pana* once more.

The Blood Moon Knights rely on their archers to attack, as two arrive and draw their arrows from their long bows. The archers shoot their arrows and I evade one of them, but the other arrow strikes me in my leg, leaving only a flesh wound. "Arrgh!" I scream. It is painful, but my adrenaline numbs it.

I pull out my arrow and quickly shoot at the archers, immobilizing one of them.

Right as the knights approach, ready to ambush me, I get to my feet and see the body of a large creature plummeting down toward us like a meteor. *It is the Manananggal!* It's large body hurdles toward the group of knights, knocking most of them to the ground. *Ulap* and Princess Nadya appear behind me, Nadya's large whip lashing at the archers, striking down their bows. I attack and stun the archers with my sword. *Ulap* lets out a blaring neigh and gallops toward the *Manananggal* ramming its large body. The blow sends the bat creature into the waters of the lake.

The *Manananggal* emerges from the water, barely able to flap its wings. It tries to stretch them and fly back into the air, but lets out another loud screech and stumbles away, defeated, into the forest.

"That's our *Ulap*! Let that *Manananggal* know who the real King of the Forest is!"

Ulap lets out a triumphant neigh that sounds much like laughter.

"Looks liked you needed some help, fellow warrior," Nadya says.

"*Salamat*, Nadya," I yell back.

Aysha and Nami dash toward the fallen warriors, rendering them immobile with their extract-drenched blades. *I can't believe it. We were winning!* I wrap the gash of my wound with another piece of cloth, the adrenaline of the battle still flowing within me.

I see Father standing in the open field, calm and collected, a smug look on his face. *It is time he finally gets what he deserves.* Just as I am ready to attack him, he raises the Serpent's Dagger into the air. He then stabs the dagger onto the sacred soil of the Enchanted Lake's grass and takes a few steps back. I stagger backwards as an earthquake begins to rumble the ground.

What is he up to? A flash of lightning strikes the dagger and a blast of light surges from it, creating an even larger earthquake. I see a light emerge from the dagger and watch it transform into to a new shape...a *Naga*!

Father bows down to the ground, "Oh Deity of Eclipses, we have brought you back to the sacred lands of your home. We are ready to serve you, Great *Bakunawa*," he says.

The Bakunawa! She stands in front of me, the Serpent's Dagger in her hand; her ominous and threatening aura creates pressure in the atmosphere. She is beautiful beyond what I imagined. Her serpent tail is of a deep, royal violet. Her scales glimmer in the moonlight and are shaped like fangs. She is large, almost twice as tall as I am. Her long black hair whips in the air from the sudden gusts of wind created by her transformation. I stare into her glowing eyes, lost in a trance. *I understand why someone so beautiful and powerful as Bakunawa is venerated so highly by the Blood Moon Knights and the Temple Keepers.*

She looks dangerous, but I know she will not be impossible to defeat. At least, not until she transforms again into a serpent dragon. I look up at the sky, and see the Full Moon, nearly completely red. *She must have disguised herself as the dagger to hide until the right time. All this time she was under our noses! The blood bond ritual of the final ceremony was her way of controlling the Blood Moon Knights. Once they cut their palms with the Serpent's Dagger, they must have fallen under her control, just like Ate Lanie. So cunning and devious—no wonder she is a great threat.*

She is silent but even without speaking, her presence is magnificent, that I, too, cannot speak. *This is my chance!* I quickly prepare my *pana*, and with only a few arrows left, I draw my bow, hoping *Ate Lanie*'s concoction will be strong enough paralyze the *Bakunawa*. I aim at her and notice that she is staring at me, our eyes locked, daring me to shoot her.

I will my hands to move, but they feel as though they are tethered to the bow—my fingers frozen unable to let go. I am too shocked to be in the presence of the Deity of Eclipses. *I almost swore my loyalty to serve her for my entire life. She is really here.* Before I get a chance to launch my arrow, Father leaps in front of me.

"Not so fast!" he says as he strikes his blade, his sword cutting my arrowhead. Father's attack wakes me from my trance.

The *Bakunawa* looks right toward the shrine and makes her way toward it, slithering fast toward the lake. *She is going to catch up with Mala once they get the mask and destroy it!* I must stop her, but Father is in the way.

"We got her!" yells Nadya. *Ulap* dashes full force toward the *Bakunawa*. She is fast, but not as fast as the *Tikbalang*. The Beast King catches up to her and, with his mighty claws, he slashes toward her. The Deity of Eclipses blocks the blow with her dagger, but the momentum of the blow causes her to fall backwards. *Ulap* gets atop the *Bakunawa,* and he stomps his hooves heavily on the *Bakunawa*'s serpent tail. Her scales protect her like armor. Nadya strikes at the *Bakunawa*, hitting her forearms. The *Bakunawa* hisses in frustration. The deity slams her tail on the ground, causing a great earthquake on the sacred land. The rumble of the ground causes *Ulap* to lose his hold on her, and she escapes his grasp. I fall to the ground, as well, and watch

Father stumble, too. On equal footing, the *Bakunawa* and the Beast King continue to clash. Nadya lets out a cry as she aids *Ulap* with her whip.

Father charges at me with his sword. "You will pay for this, Salem!" yells Father, his voice stinging my ears.

"Pay for what? Your tombstone?" I say, drawing my sword preparing for battle.

Father slashes his sword toward me. I parry his attack and our swords meet. I feel the resistance of his blade against mine as I try to push against his strength, but Father is strong. Aysha and Nami attempt to help with their spears.

"No! This is my fight!" I tell them. "This is between just you and me, Father. I'll prove to you that I am the better warrior."

Our blades deflect. Instead of coming toward him, I step back and prime a defensive stance. I take a deep breath and watch Father's footwork. *Father is stronger, so I need to be light on my feet.* I dodge each strike, like a dance, allowing my senses to guide the directions of my steps.

"You will never be me," says Father.

"You're right. I would never want to be a person that abandons their own family—a father who tries to hurt his own children. Mother would be ashamed!" I say.

I see Father's face filled with rage at the thought of Mother. *That is his pain point!* As he attacks me once more, I move left to evade and strike my sword at him. Father dodges and knocks me down, his punch knocking me to the ground. The blow is heavy on my face. I get up and wipe the blood off my mouth.

"You know nothing of your mother. You are a failure of a son!"

"Failure?" I yell as I strike him, "If Mother could see you now!"

Father shakes his head, his frustrations becoming more evident. He speeds toward me, and I watch him carefully. He strikes to my left. I dodge right and maneuver to grab his wrist and disarm him of his blade, I punch him with my other hand. I hit right into his lower jaw, causing him to tumble backwards to the ground.

I move toward him and with my sword, I bring the edge of the blade up to his neck. "You're the true failure, Father. I know she would never continue to love a man who couldn't love his own children!"

"Killing me will not save you from the *Bakunawa*'s wrath. Her revenge will be secured," he says, the madness in his blood shot eyes sickening me. *I know deep down within me that this is not his fault. He is under the spell of the Serpent's Dagger. The Deity of Eclipse's spite and vengeance is like a poison. I could have easily been like Father if I were initiated, myself. I can't kill him.*

"Grab him!" I tell the *Taal* Warriors. Nami and Aysha quickly come to my aid and stun him with their blades, cutting a small gash on his right arm and leaving him paralyzed. I pull my sword away from his neck. Father is still able to speak, "See, you couldn't go through with it. You think you are like them. You are no true warrior, but still a coward," he says.

I take a moment and stare Father right in his eyes, "The way of the warrior is not always driven through death and anger. That is not my warrior way. I learned from the *Taal* warriors to have respect for life and balance. If being a coward leaves me with my honor, then so be it."

I make my way over toward the shrine. As I approach, I realize Mala's physical body is nowhere to be found. *Where did they go?*

Nearby, toward the Enchanted Lake's shores, I see *Ulap* exhausted from the *Bakunawa*'s attacks, the pace of his strides slowing down. I hear his loud breaths. He tries to let out a neigh but does not roar as mightily due to the fatigue from the fight. Nadya looks to be at her limit as well. "Charge!" she yells, her trusted whip ready. *Ulap* tries to gallop over, but his slow movements cause him to react poorly to the *Bakunawa*'s attack. She evades him and wraps her large serpent tail around him, forming a constricting coil and subduing his body. *Bakunawa* cuts *Ulap* with her Serpent's Dagger, creating a scar attempting to turn the Beast King into one of her minions.

Nadya topples to the ground. "No!" I yell, running over to grab Nadya as she stumbles toward me.

"Princess Nadya! Are you okay?" I ask.

Nadya coughs and slowly manages to get up. "The *Bakunawa* is too powerful. We have to save *Ulap*!" She readies her whip to fight the deity.

I stop her from moving forward. I can't allow her to get hurt. It is too late, the *Bakunawa* has stabbed *Ulap* with the dagger.

"What are you doing? Let me go! *Ulap*!" she yells.

I continue to hold her back. We can't fight the *Bakunawa* head on like this.

"No!" Nadya shrieks. Losing *Ulap* to the hands of the *Bakunawa* isn't easy for the princess, especially after forging their new, strong bond. If the Beast King is under the *Bakunawa*'s control, we lose.

Ulap's body is still on the ground. The *Bakunawa* unravels her serpent tail, smiling, ready for the *Tikbalang* to be in her full control. I grab hold of Nadya, who tries to push me off. I know she wants to reach *Ulap*, but it's too late.

Ulap finally gets up. He turns toward us, and I prepare my *pana* and arrow, ready to fire. *Ulap* stares at us, his eyes sharp.

He lets out a neigh, the pressure of his breath blows a gust into our faces. He suddenly lunges, but instead of jumping at us, he thrusts his body at the *Bakunawa* and rams her into the ground. The deity hisses in pain at the blow. *The dagger didn't work on him! But why?*

Nadya laughs in relief, "That's right! I am the true master of the *Tikbalang*—because I pulled his golden mane, he only obeys me. He is a beast of madness, your chaos cannot control him, *Bakunawa!*" She readies her whip to fight alongside her companion. I ready my sword, as well.

The *Bakunawa* lets out a frightening hiss and slashes one of *Ulap*'s eyes, causing him to fall back to the ground, neighing in pain from the blow. The *Bakunawa* takes this chance to escape the fight and slithers from the shore. Quickly, she submerges her serpent body into the depths of the Enchanted Lake. We run to *Ulap*. With heavy breaths, he manages to neigh. His left eye is blinded from the dagger and his body droops from the tiresome battle.

"You did well, my king of the forest," says Nadya, petting his head.

"*Salamat, Ulap,* you are one of the bravest warriors I know," I say. *But why did the Bakunawa run away?*

Then, I look up and notice that the total lunar eclipse has arrived. The Moon is tinted in a deep crimson red, bleeding in the night sky. *She didn't run away. She must have withdrawn to the water to complete her transformation, drawing her full power from the Blood Moon and absorbing the powerful lakas energy of the Enchanted Lake.*

At first there is no movement, but then the ground shakes violently and erupts. The lake is no longer calm and serene but made of tsunamis crashing viciously across the waters. The sapphire blue waters boil, huge bubbles and steam forming on the surface. The visible mist is accompanied by a wave of heat, filling the air, causing us all to sweat. Then, the sapphire waters transition to a much darker, red color. It looks as though blood has stained the sacred lake.

She's coming.

As the Earth continues to quake and the blood red tsunamis crash in the boiling water, a great serpent dragon erupts from the lake like a volcano. The colossal dragon is almost as big as the size of the lake, itself, propelling herself straight toward the night sky. With great speed, the *Bakunawa* darts above us all, like an arrow aimed toward the Moon, her purple serpent body is the only thing I see as she leaves us in her destructive rouse.

We were too late.

CHAPTER 12

HALIYA'S SECRET

───────

Mala

As I descend into the waters following the *Naga* sisters, I feel the vibrations and energy within the lake's sacred blue waters. All around me, the sensations of the lake are cool and refreshing. Although I am in my astral projection, the *lakas* that lives within the lake is rich and intense.

I sense the strong power of *lakas* like never before. *Maybe because I am exposed in my spirit state, the flow of energy that I feel is amplified, too. The songs of the water, the plant life and animals that live peacefully here, remind me of the forest trail back in Zambo.*

As we swim deeper, I can see the different ecosystems of flora and fauna that exist within the lake. We pass through a forest of kelp trees, the large brown algae dense in groupings and home to octopi, fish, and crabs. Swimming freely underwater, I feel that I am in an entirely different world.

I enjoy the scenery of pristine coral reefs. Colonies of different colors crowd the bottom of the lake, the sand below them glowing like stars. The scenery is immaculate, reflecting the pure state of the water's *lakas* energy. Fish pop their heads out of the coral reefs, curious to see us swim by their stony homes. Then suddenly, I feel a huge aura coming toward us. *What could be big enough to live in this lake? Is it the Bakunawa?*

As the aura nears, I realize it is not one large aura, but hundreds of small ones! A large school of silver fish pass us peacefully, their scales shining gracefully under the reflection of the moonlight. Their vibrations are collective and in harmony, like their auras are all in sync. The grouping of these auras disguises them as one big aura, most likely to protect themselves from their predators.

When we reach the depths of the Enchanted Lake, I look up and see the full Moon shining brightly below, its color tinted red, reminding me to hurry. As I look below, I see a grandiose but unclear construction. Once we arrive at the bottom of the lake, the structure becomes much more visible. What lies there, open, is the most elaborate and ancient tomb. Looking into the dark openings of the tomb, I hear whispers. I can't make out the whispers in my head, but I feel them from within the temple calling to me.

"Welcome to our home," says Hydrophis.

As we swim inside the underwater temple, I sense strong magical energy seeping from within the *Naga*'s abode, a generator of ancient spiritual energy. This must be the source of the Enchanted Lake's *lakas* that feeds into the rest of the island. I caress the ancient granite of the tomb, feeling the vibrations of many different auras. *Do the spirits of the dead reside here?* I focus my senses to commune with the bonded spirits that reside in the tomb but get no answer. I keep swimming.

I remember the structure of this temple. *Yes, it reminds me of the Temple of Serpents back at Zambo. I see that even the Bakunawa didn't forget her own roots.* The roofs of the temple are held by statue shafts, each statue resembling the image of a *Naga*, their stances strong and faces benevolent. I wonder how *Bakunawa* could have been so angry to have become so violent.

Hydrophis notices my curiosity as I observe the linings of the tomb, "This temple is known as The Eternal Graves," she says.

"Graves? Is this a burial ground?" I ask.

"Our temple resembles a grave, but it is not a resting place for the bodies of the dead," answers Oligodon.

"In this tomb lies the secrets of the dead. We protect the secrets of those who have passed. These secrets manifest as treasures or lost possessions," says Samar.

"They reside here, to never be forgotten, just like the *Haliya*'s Mask of Gold," I say, "I understand now, the energy I was feeling earlier within the tomb's walls were not spirits of the dead, but their leftover *lakas* residue from their past lives still strong within their treasures."

"That's right, we are the protectors of those secrets. Here, nothing is lost or forgotten, even if a soul passes to the Underworld or is reborn into a new life, their treasures lie here, guarded, each in their own Sanctum of Secrets," says Hydrophis.

"Each treasure has their own sacred place. The Mask of Gold is this way," mentions Oligodon, pointing into a corridor where the walls are lined in gold. Then I hear it again, the whispers calling me from the end of the corridor. The *Nagas* lead the way toward them. The closer we get to the end of the corridor, the clearer the whispers become. I finally hear it, a voice I do not recognize but does sound like a distant memory. "Remember the spell," whispers the voice. *But what could it mean?*

The golden corridor comes to a dead end. A large circular gate made of solid gold sits at the end of the passageway. I see my distorted reflection in the gold. Inscriptions of symbols are carved on the door surface. *It is Baybayin!* I read the text and it is the same as the prophecy of the copperplate inscription:

"Death's door resides in the waters of sirens; one must venture to the Nagas' sacred island;

And in those waters lies the treasure of old; A lunar legacy forged of gold;

A champion of two souls made to seal the eclipse of its wrongdoing; shall bring a new hope through honest fate and challenged pursuing."

"I think *Haliya*'s secret is calling me to open the door," I say as I swim toward the gate. I touch its golden surface and feel a strong protective energy pouring from inside the gate. Its presence reminds me of a waterfall. It is hard to push against this energy. The protective magic is repelling and forcing back anything to protect what it hides inside.

"Do you feel the strong lunar energy?" asks Hydrophis.

"Yes, I do."

"The Golden Moon's power has protected the treasure hidden inside so strongly that even we could never access or open this gate once it was sealed," says Oligodon.

"She must've cast a protective barrier spell to protect the Mask of Gold from *Bakunawa*," I say.

"If you are the true lunar legacy, you can open the gate," says Samar.

"But how?" I ask.

"Only the champion knows. I am afraid this is the most help we can give you. Only you can open the gate from here," says Hydrophis.

I have to stay composed. Haliya would have left a clue. I re-read the *Baybayin* script again. *A champion of two souls made to seal the eclipse of its wrongdoing.*

A champion of two souls. That must mean me—my soul and *Haliya's,* as one. *Made to seal the eclipse of its wrongdoing. Seal the eclipse. The Bakunawa must be the eclipse, and we seal her power with the Mask of Gold?*

Okay, yes but how do we get the Mask of Gold first? Come on, Mala think! Then the voice echoes in my head again, calling from within the door, "Remember the spell." *I don't know any spell. I don't remember. Maybe...maybe it's not my memory I need to interrogate—a champion of two souls.*

If I am also Haliya, then I must have access to her memories—those of my past life. But how can I reach out to my past life's memories? What would Ate Lanie do? Lakas cannot be used fully. It is only borrowed, the flow of our lifeforce lives on through new forms and can be converted, manipulated, or transformed.

That's right, she would draw her energy from the spirit and allow it to flow inside of her—just as I did with Kalma when I let his wisdom flow inside of me. I did the same with Ulap, too.

I put my hands onto the gate and feel the rush of energy flow again, the remnants of *Haliya's* celestial power still alive. I take a deep breath and close my eyes. From the palms of my hands, I allow the energy to flow right into me, absorbing the powers of the Moon. I open my eyes, see my astral projection glow silver in the light, reflected in the golden gate. My eyes shine a bright golden yellow, like the stars. The person I see before me reminds me of the woman from my dream. I close my eyes again.

Remember the spell.

I see *Haliya* in the field of flowers. She is sitting in the middle of the field; her eyes fill with tears of amber that drip down her face. I cannot hear her or anything. The memories are silent, but I feel her presence, her feelings. I understand her mind; I become a bystander in my past, watching the memories she wants me to see. Her tears, at first, are pure molten gold falling into her hands. Then the remnants of her tears in her palms begin to take shape. Her tears forge themselves into a mask. *The Mask of Gold!*

As I walk closer to inspect the mask, I see *Haliya*, but she cannot see me. Every detail of the intricate design and lavish aura emanates from the mask. Five spades sprout on the mask's forehead, like triangles forming a crown-like heading. The mask has a golden gem centered in the middle of the forehead, slightly above and between the eyes. I recognize a deep sadness behind the beauty, as well—the sadness of *Haliya*'s pain and sorrow in its creation.

She suddenly wears the mask, her golden spear and silver blade in each hand ready for battle. I watch *Bulan* approach, his amethyst eyes in tears, yelling at her, begging her not to go. But *Haliya* must seek vengeance for her fallen siblings. Their deaths could not be in vain.

The visions of the memories now warp into a new environment. We are back in the Enchanted Lake. The Blood Moon is glowing a deep crimson red as *Haliya* descends from the heavens. The Enchanted Lake boils blood red water, like lava in a volcano. A great and giant sea serpent dragon emerges from the lake, her body and head almost as big as the entire lake. *The Bakunawa! So, this was her dragon form in the eclipse.* The dragon's face is monstrous and resembles that of a crocodile's head, with whiskers tailing down on the bottom of her jaw. On the side of her dragon face are large gills that stretch open like large fans, making her look more intimidating and ferocious. The dragon's deep crimson red eyes fill with rage. The dragon's wide-gaping mouth holds a red tongue oozing with acid saliva. I see large fangs in her mouth as well, the size of obelisk statues and just as fierce as the *Manananggal's fangs.*

Haliya stands her ground and points her golden spear right at the *Bakunawa*. I feel her rage—her anger and resolve for vengeance power her lunar *lakas.* Their divine auras clash so powerfully that earthquakes shake the island and hurricane winds whirl throughout the trees and villages. There, she challenges the *Bakunawa,* and the epic Great Battle of Moons has begun, leaving natural disasters in its wake. The Great Battle of Moons does nothing but destroy life around it and create imbalance on the *Isla Sirena.* Years have passed and the island is still healing from the effects of this lunar eclipse. *Will I have to do this, too, to save our islands and our people?*

The memory changes after the battle, *Haliya* and the *Bakunawa* are both gravely wounded. The Blood Moon passes, and the total lunar eclipse subsides, causing the great serpent dragon to transform back into her *Naga* form. Defeated, the *Bakunawa* flees the *Isla Sirena,* disappearing into the ocean depths. *Haliya* is dying from her wounds and cannot chase after her enemy. Exhausted from the battle, she plummets into the Enchanted Lake, sinking to the bottom of the waters. There, Hydrophis, Samar, and Oligodon find *Haliya* and carry her body into the Temple of the Eternal Graves.

I could feel *Haliya*'s time was running out and she knows this memory is ending, as well. She is alone in the Sanctum of Secrets. She places the Mask of Gold onto a statue in the room. Using what little divinity she has left, she seals the sanctum and creates a golden gate. *Haliya*'s spell is the *Chant of the Golden Moon*. She looks into the reflection of the golden gate, and I see myself behind her. She smiles and touches the reflection of me and closes her eyes.

I remember.

I open my eyes and am brought back to the present. I feel immense grief from *Haliya*'s memories. *I hear the whispers of my past refuse to forget her legacy.* But the thought strikes me again, *Why me?* Then I remember *Sidapa*'s voice ringing in my head, *"Being you is a gift, is it not? Wishes come true to the destined who are brave enough to chase them."*

For now, I need to trust in myself and in my truth. I am not an imposter in my own body. I belong here and now, as Mala, the lunar legacy.

"I remember it now, the *Chant of the Golden Moon*," I tell the *Nagas*, "She originally cast it as a protection spell to protect the Mask of Gold. Before her passing, she used the last of her strength to create this gate. By repeating the chant and channeling her aura, I can manipulate the *lakas* she left behind to unbind the spell."

I touch my palms to the gate and the flow of the energy pours inside of me. The whisper returns to my head and I recognize the voice of *Haliya*. Our voices fuse together and we repeat the chant, as if *Haliya* is speaking through me:

"This gate is my shield, my secret sealed to protect;

Until a heart of gold shall arrive, whose spirit of mine will reflect

the past and present of the Golden Moon which is thee;
Who will bear the mask once again to set us all free;
The lunar legacy of the prophecy, who is both of daughter
and of son;
In my death this gate is created, and in my new life it shall
be undone."

Suddenly, I feel a surge of *lakas* energy blast from within the gate, the pressure from the seal propelling itself as the gate begins to open. There, finally, is a room covered in gold. I see the artifact I have fought so hard to find. The mask is mounted in the middle of the room and inside the mouth of a large statue of a *Naga*'s head. The mouth is open, and the mask sits on top of its tongue, shining brightly in the gleaming light of the room. The energy of the mask is strong. I feel the beauty of its strength and sadness—*Haliya*'s protected treasure. *My protected treasure, too.* As I approach closer to the mask, I feel it calling to me. I get the urge to put it on but cannot do so in my astral form. *One of the Nagas can carry it back above to the surface.* Looking closer, I see that the mask is almost as flawless as it was in *Haliya*'s memory, except for a scar clearly visible on its left side. *This imperfection only adds to the mask's beauty. She fought with honor and fought to the death giving it her all for her siblings and to keep the balance of this world.*

"It's beautiful, just like you," praised Samar.

"Yes, it is. Put it on, already," urges Oligodon.

At first I am confused. *How can I touch the mask in my astral state?* I grab hold of the mask with my two hands.

"I'm in my astral projection, how am I touching the mask?" I ask.

"The Mask of Gold is an extension and a combination of your past life's spiritual and physical body. Because it is a part of you, you can hold it in this spiritual state," answers Hydrophis. The mask is made of *Haliya's* very own golden tears which make them my own tears, too. *I don't think I'll get used to the idea that I was a deity in my past life.*

I put on the mask and it fits perfectly. The power of the mask evokes a sense of reminiscence. It belongs to me, like a piece of my life that was missing throughout my lifetime has finally returned. I feel the enhanced power of the lunar *lakas* from the mask amplifying my spirit.

"Quickly! The total lunar eclipse of the Blood Moon is almost here!" warns Samar.

"Yes, I need to return to my physical body and finish the Great Battle of Moons once and for all," I say.

We swim out of the Temple of Eternal Graves, and back onto the surface of the lake.

Oh no! I see the battle has begun. Salem is in the midst of combat with Father. Then, suddenly a flash of lightning strikes the ground and Father's dagger transforms into the *Bakunawa* in her *Naga* form. The Deity of Eclipses immediately looks over to me and sees my astral projection in the lake as I wear the Mask of Gold. I feel her energy shift. Threatened, she slithers toward me. *I need to hurry to my body.* It is a race against time. I rush in flight toward the Shrine of Seven Moons. I see *Ulap* dash toward *Bakunawa*, Nadya at his side, and they attack her. This buys me more time. My astral projection finally arrives and realigns itself to my physical body—the Mask of Gold fits onto my face.

I open my eyes, ready for battle, but am no longer in the Shrine of Seven Moons by the Enchanted Lake. *No, this is a familiar place.* I look and see the purple flowers and surrounding fields of the large garden. *The Takay Flower garden in my dream!* A butterfly flies by me, the same one with its long-tail ends. Like in my dream, I follow it once more. I am led to the marble mirror and the butterfly dissolves, sparkling silver glitter, into the mirror. I look at my reflection. This time I only see myself. There I am, my face adorned by the Mask of Gold, but I can see my deep and luminous dark brown eyes. My long, dark wavy hair wisps in the air like before, as if gravity disappears. In the reflection, I suddenly see a silver body appear behind me.

"With such beauty, grace, and strength, I expect no less from you," says the voice.

I look back and this time I can clearly see him, the beautiful silver body glowing like the Moon: *Bulan*. He is fit and slim with broad shoulders, but his body is petite. His demeanor is calm, reminding me of the masculine wisdom of *Kalma*. This calmness is solemn and majestic, yet he also gives off a softness; a great delicacy that seems fragile to the touch. He wears a golden crown and a transparent white-silk veil that hangs over his head, covering his face. His bright amethyst eyes glow from behind the veil. I take in his sharp facial features. He has a youthful appearance, but his beauty stems from his tranquil essence. He reminds me of sweet dreams, the kind I always wish I can cherish longer. He wears a lavender and royal purple robe that wraps across his shoulder down to his bottom half waistline. His white, long hair reaches the bottom of his feet. He is divine.

"Finally, you are home, *Ate*," he says.

CHAPTER 13

MALAYA

Mala

Bulan closes his eyes and smiles as his celestial silver body approaches me. He hugs me. At first, I stand still, feeling his heavenly vibrations. I sense his benevolent energy radiate, his aura warm and pure, much like Salem's. My arms slowly lift themselves to wrap around and hug him back. Although it is my first time meeting him, *Bulan*'s presence does not feel strange. No, this meeting feels like a long-awaited reunion.

"Finally, you have returned. I have been waiting for you for so long, *Ate*. But now you look different. May I call you *Ate*?" asks *Bulan* as he looks down at me, his brilliant amethyst eyes gleaming.

I nod. Hearing *Bulan* call me *Ate* feels right. "Yes, but I also go by Mala, now," I say.

"Of course, Mala of *Zambo*. I have been watching you from above ever since you awakened your inner gift," he says.

I look around at the endless garden, the purple *Takay Flowers* cover every spot in the soil. They are lined in silver light like in my dream. "Where am I, *Bulan*? You said this is our home...but this looks like my dream."

"This is the Moon," he says.

"The M-Moon?" I stammer. *How can I even be here right now?*

"Yes, *Ate*," *Bulan* smiles at my confusion. "The mask you're wearing brought you here. It holds special properties that even I do not understand..." He trails off, lost in my eyes. "*Haliya* was so special."

"So, I'm really here," I say.

Bulan laughs mildly and he covers his mouth with his hand, "Yes, you are really here. This is one of the many realms that exist across our vast universe. This is our home, the upper realm known as *Kaluwalhatian*, the World of Glory."[34]

"The realm above the skies..." I whisper to myself, allowing my eyes to wander away from *Bulan*'s beauty. "Can you tell me more about our home?"

"This place carries so much of our history. We were born here, amongst the planets and the stars. Before there were seven Moons, the splendor of our siblings each owned their own Moon, as well. Each of our Moons had a garden of flowers that wrapped around the entire rock. Our Moons are great sources of *lakas* energy known as the lunar *lakas*. We draw our power from our Moons. The flowers in our respective gardens were made from the colors of our eyes. That is why we called *Haliya* the Golden Moon—hers were made of golden chrysanthemums. But like our bodies glow silver, our flowers too emanate that same light resonating from the lunar *lakas*."

So this is why the Moon glows silver at night, it reflects the light emitted from the lakas, "So, this must be your Moon then."

---

34   Kaluwalhatian – World of Glory; Realm above the skies; the heavens

"Sadly, this is last Moon holding the balance of the Earth and our realm in place. I have been here, alone, for many years," he says with a defeated tone.

"Tell me, brother, of our time together in my past life," I say to try and cheer him up.

Immediately, the purple light in his eyes shine and his spirit lifts, "I used to bother you all the time—coming onto your Moon, bringing you into my shenanigans. But we were all connected, the seven of us, a family together that orbited around the Earth."

His spirit is so gentle and sweet, and his playfulness reminds me so much of Salem. *Kuya* would always barge into my room too, whether it was because he was eager for me to try out a new dish or tell me stories from his day training with the knights.

"You know, out of our other siblings, *Haliya* was my twin. But she was always so strong, the bravest of us all. That's why I called her *Ate*. She always looked out for me, even to the end, no matter how hard I tried to convince her not to challenge the *Bakunawa*. I have always felt that violence was not the answer. And now she lives through you, the champion of two souls, Mala of *Zambo*."

Salem looked after me growing up. Salem was my role model and I learned so much from him. It is funny to hear how I was the bigger sibling as *Haliya* and was able to influence *Bulan*. I relate to *Bulan*—we taught our older siblings empathy.

"When orbiting around the Earth, my siblings and I have many important functions: pulling the tides of the waters, stabilizing the ground with our gravity, and providing life on Earth with light at night. You should have seen how bright the night sky looked from Earth with seven Moons. It was a grand sight! All in all, our main purpose as the Moon deities was to provide balance between our realms."

Balance. I begin to really see and understand our role in nature and as spirits of the *Kaluwalhatian* realm. Although we belong in the World of Glory, we have a sacred duty and obligation to protect the balance of life between our realms and the spirits that inhabit them.

But how lonely he must have been all these years. Why did Haliya have to leave Bulan behind? How could she let her anger and need for revenge get the best of her? Her fight against the Bakunawa did not bring this needed balance to the islands or our home here above the skies.

Was this the point of my rebirth? To find a new answer? To take a better direction that my past life could not?

"I'm so sorry for leaving you here all alone," I say as I grab *Bulan*'s hands and rub them gently, "I remember how scared you were the night *Haliya* left to fight the *Bakunawa*."

He grabs my hands back and holds them tight. "It's okay, I understand why you did it. But you're back now, reborn as a magnificent human—a *Babaylan* of all things," he giggles. "I have always appreciated humanity. Their love is so precious. They were one of the reasons I enticed you and our siblings to visit Earth in the first place! Our curiosity got the best of us in the end." He shrugs, "But I haven't been alone all the time, I hear the prayers of the people on Earth. They give me the strength to protect myself."

"Yes, the prayers from the Shrine of Seven Moons. I remember *Ate Lanie* mentioned the shrine is a sacred place where she and the people used to pray to you," I say.

"Our siblings and I used to hear all the prayers from people across many islands. Shrines acts as doors from Earth to the divine realms, but ever since the rise of the *Bakunawa*, many of our lunar shrines have been destroyed and forgotten. The Shrine of Seven Moons is one of the last ones standing. Each and every prayer reached me from that shrine. I felt everything so deeply: their love, hopes and dreams, and even their sadness, grief, and pain. Their faith in me gave me purpose and strength."

I am glad to hear *Bulan* had people to give him hope.

"But in recent years, as you know, the prayers that gave me the power to protect myself diminished. My power has grown weaker, and I'm no longer able to defend myself against the *Bakunawa*. The balance of our universe is now in your hands."

As much as I want to sit here and be with *Bulan*, reminiscing with him about my past life, I sense the shift of energy around us. The *lakas* of the Moon is transforming. I look around me and slowly, the silver light of the *Takay Flowers* vanishes. Their luminescence becomes dark red, one after the other, until the richness of the red hue covers the lavender color of the *Takay Flower* entirely. All I can see is an ocean of scarlet flowers across the endless garden. Just like the flowers, *Bulan*'s silver glow turns bright red.

"The time of Blood Moon is here," says *Bulan*. *The dire time to face the Bakunawa has come.*

I finally feel her—the *Bakunawa*, her strong intense *lakas* so powerful that I sense the vibrations of her energy from her place on Earth. Like a cosmic meteor rushing through the night sky, I sense her massive aura bolting toward us. At first, I am scared. I remember the memories of *Haliya* and how she challenged the Great Serpent in that blood-soaked lake. *How can I be brave like Haliya?* My whole body shakes. Then, I feel *Bulan*'s hand clench onto mine as he holds me tightly. He is scared, too. I take a deep breath and try to calm down.

In this lifetime, I am no longer fighting the Bakunawa alone. No, this time I have my family. I think of Salem. I know how to be confident and powerful like my *kuya*. He shows me valor in his hunts and his passion for providing for and protecting others. I remember the sorrow of the Mask of Gold, and how it carries the strength and power of my befallen Moon siblings before me. I hold onto *Bulan*'s hand and think of him. He is with me and together we are stronger. *I can channel the spirits of all my siblings for this final encounter. This is my second chance.*

The red flowers of the garden dance wildly in the weightless air, scarlet petals flow with the chaotic vibrations of the *Bakunawa's lakas* aura. She finally arrives, her large violet serpent body rockets above the Moon and she looks at us from above. She belts out a large roar, the blast of it like a tidal wave of pressure. There in front of me, she looks just as she did in *Haliya's* memories. Her deep vermillion eyes glare as she looks down upon me, her large mouth and fangs gaping. Her *lakas* is overpowering and immense, filling the air. *The Great Serpent Dragon. The Moon Eater. The Deity of Eclipses.*

I glance over to see *Bulan* falling onto the ground. I try to pull him up, but he is weak and begins to breathe heavily. I feel his *lakas* slowly leaving, his flow of energy pulled and absorbed toward the *Bakunawa*.

"*Bulan!*" I yell as I try to help him. Then I feel it, too, my lifeforce slowly being sucked away. I fall onto my knees to the ground with him. My breath becomes heavy and my body slowly drains. Each second that passes begins to feel longer and slow. *Bulan's* grip slowly releases from my hand, his red light begins to fade and wither like a dying flower. The red scarlet flowers all around us began to wither, too, as each red glowing petal is pulled into the Moon Eater's jaws like a vacuum. *So, this is how she devours the Moon. She absorbs our lakas until we no longer exist.*

I can't give up. We have come too far! I try to get up, but my body feels so light I can barely stand. *I can't let the Bakunawa absorb all the power from my home.* I sense my lunar *lakas* flowing still inside of me. The power of the flow rushes like a river all throughout my body. I close my eyes and try to gather the remaining energy from the Moon. It is a battle with the *Bakunawa*, a war between us, pulling the *lakas* of the Moon, but I stand my ground.

I take a deep breath and feel the Moon's power from below the soles of my feet. I feel re-energized, like the wild vitality of a whirlpool, and I draw the surrounding lunar *lakas* toward myself, the petals circling in my current. I feel like a blooming flower, my arms like petals ready to spread, the *lakas* within me surging outward. I am the last surviving *Takay Flower*, ready to save my lunar home. *This will only last for a moment.* My whole body flashes with light. I raise my hands toward her and with great force, I blast a ray of light that shoots from the palms of my hands. The blast of moonlight hits the face of the *Bakunawa* and creates a powerful shockwave that pushes me back to the ground.

I look up to see if my attack worked. The Great Serpent stands there, stunned. For a moment, the vacuum ceases. The blast is my most powerful attack, and I don't have the fight in me to project another powerful launch. *I can't even put up a fight like Haliya. I'm not brave nor powerful like her.* I fall back on the ground, defeated. *How could I fail everyone? She is too powerful. Unstoppable.*

My head begins to feel dizzy and my line of sight blurs. I fall face-flat onto the flowers below me. *In the last moments of my life, I will stare at the scarlet Takay Flowers.* My breath slows as I try to save as much *lakas* as I can within me to survive. Tears begin to flow down my eyes. *At least I will see you again, Mother.*

I feel something touch my hand. *Bulan!* In his harsh breath, he transfers all his remaining lunar energy into me. He gives me the strength I need, a rush of confidence that powers my conviction. *I can't give up now. Bulan* still breathing heavy. He gathers up a slight smile. *I have to keep trying—keep persisting for the sake of the balance. Bulan* slowly closes his eyes and rests on the flowerbed.

"*Salamat, Bulan,*" I say as I kiss his forehead. He is barely alive. *I need to try and find a new way to stop the Bakunawa. For the sake of Salem, Bulan, Ate Lanie, Kalma, Nadya, Ulap, The people of Taal and of Zambo, Sidapa, Lolo Alma, and Mother. I can't give up now.*

With all the leftover strength I can muster, I get back up on my feet. I stare the Great Serpent right in her eyes as she rouses from her stunned state and opens her mouth. I do not try to resist her power. I recall my learnings with *Ate Lanie,* the flow of energy needs to be a balance. I recall my moment with *Ulap* and how I felt his fear. By letting him in, I was able to find balance between our spirits together. This time, I don't try to fight the *Bakunawa. No, I need to let her in and connect with her spirit. I need to be strong enough to not let her overtake me and consume me fully or else I will be lost, forever devoured by the chaos of the eclipse.*

I close my eyes and accept the flow of *lakas* from the *Bakunawa* drift within me, her *lakas* energy is formidable like a strong current, turbulent and unbreaking. Then, through the energy flowing through me, I begin to hear her song. It is painful, a profound sound of hurt. As our energies connect, I fight with her inner being. Her rage is unavoidable—the rejection of love from the Moon siblings...from *Haliya*. I finally understand her desire to kill me, to devour the Moon, a constant reminder that the Moon siblings never loved her. I felt her desire to belong and to be loved by divine creatures from the World of Glory, only to be left in the darkness of the Underworld, alone.

These emotions make her flawed, but not evil. The root of where it—the power of this darkness—comes from somewhere else.

I see now how the *Bakunawa* must feel. I, too, felt this way in the *City of Zambo*. I know the pain of being rejected by people who treat me like a monster. I know the isolation and loneliness. If it weren't for Salem, *Lolo Alma*, my books, and my inner power, I could have easily become like the *Bakunawa* myself: bitter and filled with anger because of the unfairness of the world. But to seek revenge is not the answer. Vengeance is never the answer. *Haliya* taught me that.

I begin to grow clarity in the *Bakunawa*'s *lakas* flowing with mine. *To create balance between our spirits, my resolve needs to be stronger than her plight. The only way to defeat her is not to fight her, but to heal her.*

I feel the Mask of Gold begin to glow and shine, a bright golden bursting energy. My body glows silver again, drawing power from the remnants of *Haliya* from the Mask of Gold, except this time, I repurpose the energy to project a different effect. I do this not from a resolve of vengeance or violence, but a resolve of hope and healing. Combined with the power of *Bulan*'s lunar *lakas*, I lift myself up slowly, gravity no longer holding me down as I become one with the mask. I ride the vacuum of the *Bakunawa*'s flow of energy and fly straight toward her. She continues to consume my aura, and I want her to draw this newfound power.

When I arrive near her face, I hold myself midair, repelling myself against being fully consumed. I have the power to stare her right in the eyes. She stares back at me, her intense and blazing eyes glaring fiercely like a great burning fire.

"I spent all this time afraid of your power. So filled with fear and anger at the things you have done, to my people of the islands, of *Taal*, of *Zambo*, and of my own family past and present. I wanted so badly to take away your power. To defeat you and destroy you forever. To teach you a lesson. Well, now I know that is wrong. I taught you a lesson, and it was a lesson of hate and punishment. Here *Bakunawa*, I give you my power. Take it all," I tell her. "It's time to heal you from this curse."

I take the Mask of Gold off my face. I turn it around to face the *Bakunawa*. A flash of bright golden light glows outward toward the Great Serpent's face. The *Bakunawa* roars a great howl of pain as the glow of light beams, dazzling in its heavenly grace.

"That's right, this energy you're absorbing is changing you!" I watch the mask pull itself toward her, the *lakas* energy from the mask's golden light began to wrap around the *Bakunawa*, her serpent's amaranth purple body flailing helplessly. She becomes almost entirely engulfed by my *lakas*. Our energies no longer clash as she becomes one with the mask and the power of the Moon. *If I can feel her, now she can feel me, too.*

It is an astronomical sight to behold. The *Bakunawa*'s dragon form glows a bright golden light all over, and her dragon form diminishes. As the light dissipates, the *Bakunawa* is brought back to her *Naga* form, her long luscious hair flowing freely, weightless in space. Her eyes are no longer red, but glowing white in light. The light fades away and reveals her original amber yellow eyes, those which match the Mask of Gold on her face.

"I see you," I tell her and, together, we slowly descend back onto the Moon. Her long serpent tail rests on the crimson flower bed.

Bakunawa is truly beautiful. Her *lakas* no longer sings a song of pain and overwhelming pressure. Instead, I sense her newfound feelings showering within me: her regret and longing for change. Tears begin to fall from behind the mask.

I look over to see the *Takay Flowers* returning to their magnificent silver luminescence. The Moon is restored to its natural properties; the balance of our realms returned. I notice that, even without the mask, I can still breathe in the World of Glory. *It must be because of Haliya's soul which grounds me to this realm. This is my home, too, after all.*

Immediately, I go to check on *Bulan* who is slowly recovering from his *lakas* being drained, "Are you okay?" I say.

"*Ate*, you did it!" he says, giving me a hug.

"We did it," I say, "All of us."

I look over to the *Bakunawa*. She is still and doesn't speak. Her presence is so different from her colossal *lakas* in her dragon form. As a *Naga*, her energy is magnetic and charming. I can tell my feelings reached her through the power of the Mask of Gold.

Then, *Bakunawa* slowly slithers toward me. She halts for a moment and says, "This mask…it belongs to you," and she proceeds to take it off.

"Wait!" I say. I think of the time *Lolo Alma* gave me the copperplate inscription that had belonged to his dear *Babaylan* friend, Lau. He had passed it down to me as he knew it would serve a greater purpose outside of being hidden in a box below the *Aklatan*. Now, I, too, want to pass this sacred artifact to her. "Facing you, *Bakunawa*, I was forced to face and accept my truth—my truth from within—that truth is to preserve the balance of our realms, spirit and physical. And this first must come from within myself."

I walk over to the *Bakunawa*, no longer fearful of her presence. Her *lakas* are a part of me as mine are now a part of hers. We are finally connected and understand our melodies of energy can build with each other to create a new, beautiful harmony—a harmony of healing that this world so desperately needs.

"This gift has caused me great isolation and rejection. I thought that, because of my difference, I was meant to be alone. I know now that what I have is beautiful and important. I know that others like you seek to find inner harmony and balance along the way, too. But I didn't come through this understanding alone. I had help from my chosen friends and family. I no longer want you to feel alone because of the burden of your curse, *Bakunawa*. With the mask, I fulfilled my purpose in the prophecy, and no longer need it. Why don't you keep it? Think of it as a token of good wishes. Maybe even become a new kind of Goddess," I softly say.

"*Salamat* for sharing your spirit with me. I wish I had learned this before it was too late. I had grown consumed by my pain. I had remembered meeting a darkness that amplified my rage."

"Darkness?" I ask. *I knew what I felt was real. There really was an illness or some sort of curse residing within her.*

"Yes, years ago, when I first laid eyes on the Moon siblings by the Enchanted Lake, I—along with the other spirits of the Earth and Underworld—was struck by their divine presence. I fell in love with the Golden Moon, *Haliya*. When I was rejected, I was so hurt. I crawled to the darkest depths of the Enchanted Lake to never see the light of the Moon again and face my pain. That's when I was visited by a voice."

"A voice? Do you remember, *Bakunawa*?"

"No, it all got so hazy, but after I had heard the voice, this peculiar dagger had appeared before me," she says, looking at the Serpent's Dagger in her hand. "I remember losing control over my emotions. It was like my body had hunger and thirst for revenge. Anger, envy, rage…all these negative aspects of my spirit became amplified, and then I was suddenly lost, riding on the whim of my resolve for vengeance."

The dagger reminds me of the copperplate inscription, how it was the key to awakening my lunar powers. *Was the Serpent's Dagger the key to awakening the Bakunawa's destructive power? Who would want such a dangerous thing to happen? She was a victim to her own pain for so long.*

"I'm sorry to hear that this happened to you—to lose control of yourself, of your body. The Darkness took advantage of you at your most vulnerable point. Do you have any idea of where the Darkness has gone or what this Darkness could be?"

Bakunawa shakes her head, "No, ever since that moment, I lived on to be the Deity of Eclipses, letting my rage consume islands. This Serpent's Dagger is the only thing I have that reminds me of my first encounter with it."

Yes, the sacred artifact born from Darkness, its magical properties are dangerous and unknown. It gains power from the sacrifice of others. It takes away the agency of those cut by its crimson blade.

This Darkness begins to concern me.

"For now, I believe, it is time we celebrate new beginnings. What shall you say, *Bakunawa*?"

"Now that I have reclaimed control of my life, I shall use this newfound power to heal the places that I've conquered and help create new cultures in peace. You taught me that

I can always change. With this Mask of Gold, I will carry a part of *Haliya* with me as I atone for the pain I caused with the Blood Moon Knights."

"Yes, we can create a new world—one that symbolizes the hope of keeping our traditions alive in the changing world, one where freedom is possible, and one where we can all live in peace."

"*Salamat*, Moon Child."

"Please, call me Mala. Mala of *Zambo*."

"Indeed, Mala of *Zambo*, you have shared your true feelings. Your truth and your power have freed me of my curse. Let us now heal the Earth together."

CHAPTER 14

NEW BEGINNINGS

Salem

I am worried. We couldn't stop the *Bakunawa* and Mala is still nowhere to be found. *The Deity of Eclipses must have reached the Moon by now. But I have a feeling that wherever Mala is, they were going to save the day. I trust them. We have come a long way.*

I help Nadya take care of *Ulap*'s wound. Aysha and Nami are busy tying the Blood Moon Knights, ensuring their capture. I can't help but look at the Blood Moon, it's red glow still taunting us. The waves of the Enchanted Lake continue to boil. The tides are uncontrollable and the rumble of the ground shakes beneath our feet.

I rush over to the Shrine of Seven Moons to check on *Ate Lanie*, still lost in her trance. *Kalma* continues to coo unceasingly. I grab her and carry her away from the red tides crashing by the shore. Then suddenly, my feet are no longer on the ground. We begin floating as if the Earth and our footing are no longer stabilized. I look all around me and see everyone levitating, even *Ulap*'s massive body is rising into the air.

"I can't move!" I yell.

"The Blood Moon, it must be being devoured by the *Bakunawa*!" yells Nadya, *Ulap* neighing at the distance.

I look over and see the Enchanted Lake creating a massive tsunami. I hold onto *Ate Lanie* to try and cover her. I look over to Nadya and see *Ulap* covering her in midair to protect her. I close my eyes, clutching onto *Ate Lanie*. I can't bear to look at the devastating crash of the wave. *Please, Mala... Wherever you are, I believe in you.*

A few moments pass and I feel us slowly drift down. I hold *Ate Lanie* as we land on the sacred ground of the Enchanted Lake. A light sprinkle drizzles over us from the wave. I open my eyes and see the wave dissolve away. The waters of the lake are no longer a deep crimson color but reflecting blue sapphire like before.

The Moon is still there! The Blood Moon eclipse is over.

"What happened?" asks *Ate Lanie*. I look down and see her eyes are back to normal, no longer under the *Bakunawa*'s control.

"Glad to see you awake again," I say, teary eyed as I hug her, "You were stuck in a trance caused from by the Serpent's Dagger. We thought we lost you there, forever, *Ate Lanie*."

"*Ku ku ku!* I'm sorry for the scare, young warrior," she says as she lightly pats my back. "Where is our champion?"

Good question. Where is Mala? I have no doubt that they had a part in saving the Moon. I just wish they were back here.

The copperplate inscription on the pedestal and the *Takay Flowers* surrounding us begin to glow a bright sliver light. The sacred shrine seems to be activating somehow. From the dark blue sky, the moonlight shines on the Shrine of Seven Moons. Then I see them, Mala, their dark brown hair drifting in the air, descending from the heavens. The silver Moon shines directly behind them as if they had come from the Moon, itself. Two other beings follow behind Mala. The *Bakunawa* was one of them, in her *Naga* form, wearing the Mask of Gold, her serpent tail slithering in the air as she makes her way down to the shrine. The other being has a glowing silver body and wears a purple silk robe, covered in a white transparent veil. Like Mala, his hair also suspended in the air, silver and white in color, amethyst eyes shining. The three supreme beings land next to the pedestal of the shrine.

I get up from the ground and rush over to Mala, giving them a huge hug, "Mala you did it, you saved the day! But, where were you? What happened?" I have so many questions, but I am grateful they are okay.

They smile back at me and answer, "Sorry, *Kuya*. I had to go away for a bit, but I was accompanied by these two, so I wasn't alone. We are back now, better than ever," they say. I notice a tremendous change in Mala. They look stronger and more confident. It is powerful to see, and I am so proud of them. I rub their head with my fist and tell them, "I knew you could do it, *Ading*!"

Mala isn't the only one who I can tell has changed. I see the *Bakunawa*, as well, except her presence feels different. Her beauty is divine and her amaranth purple skin and scales shine. Her bright yellow eyes no longer project fear or pressure. I feel hopeful around her. She nods her head at me, and I nod back.

The other silver being, I don't recognize. He looks over to me with a gentle smile, "So you must be the *Kuya*, Salem. It is great to meet you. I can see my *Ate* had a great *Kuya* growing up in her new life," he says, grabbing my hand.

"*Salamat*, yes, and you are?" I ask.

"Oh, forgive me, I am Mala's other brother from their past life. I am *Bulan*, the Deity of the Last Moon."

"Right, wow!" I say, giggling at the thought. It is so shocking I just have to laugh. I look over to Mala, who just shrugs. *At this point, anything is possible.* "Well, nice to meet a fellow sibling of my hero, *Ading*."

"Indeed, and a pleasure to see the reputable older brother who took the very best care of our champion hero," he says to me.

Nadya and *Ulap* also arrive at the shrine. Aysha and Nami follow, holding Father between them. At the sight of him, I curl my fist. I take a deep breath, still angry and upset at him for his betrayal. I glare at him, but his eyes do not meet mine.

"Come, Salem," Mala says as they walk over to Father. "We can untie him," they tell the *Taal* warriors.

"No! Mala, what are you doing? He's dangerous!" I say, but they keep untying the rope. I move forward to stop them, but Mala proceeds to give Father a hug. At first Father stands still, his head down, but then he hugs Mala back. *The paralyzing cassava must have worn off.* I am confused. *Why would Mala do this? What has changed in Father?*

The *Bakunawa* approaches me and explains, "Your Father was poisoned by my sickness. The Serpent's Dagger made him lose control over his mind and body. But the bond he had with me has been destroyed now."

Ate Lanie walks over as well and places a hand over my shoulder, "Go, see your Father again," she says.

I slowly walk over to Mala and Father. Father sees me and lifts his head up. He stares at me and extends his arm outward, "Come here, my son," he says, his voice cracking slightly.

I join them in a family embrace. Tears come down my eyes. *Our Father has finally returned to us.*

"This is healing," says *Bulan*.

"Yes, this is the work I will set out to do—to right the wrongs of my Darkness," says *Bakunawa*.

After embracing our Father, I notice Mala looking toward the shore. They point, "*Bulan*, look." A dark black shape appears on the shore. It looks like a portal surrounded by black moths. A moth flutters over and lands on my hand. I look over to the portal and watch a large, muscular man emerge. He is draped in a fine red silk robe, his rich dark skin lined in white tattoos. He wears golden ornaments all around his body. On his head sits a crown of gold with horns, his black smoky hair wisps in the darkness of the night.

"My love," says the being.

Bulan gasps and runs toward the being, falling into his arms. "My *Sidapa*, my king of the Afterlife." *King of the Afterlife? The Deity of Death!*

The two stare at each other deeply. *Sidapa* caresses *Bulan*'s face and whispers, "My Moon, my beloved treasure. No matter the distance, I know my love reached you as you laid shining with the stars. My forever." The two kiss under the moonlight.

They must have been separated for a long time, yet their feelings never wavered. What a beautiful sight, I am happy for them. I look over to Nadya who, too, is in tears. She glances at me and blushes. She wipes her tears and gives me a light laugh. I smile and laugh back at the princess, too, my heart feeling warm.

"Finally, we are reunited once again in our favorite place," says *Sidapa*.

Sidapa looks over toward us. "*Maraming Salamat*, Mala and Salem of *Zambo*. You have brought my lover back to me safely. We shall finally have our long-awaited *honeymoon*," he says as he carries *Bulan*.

"*Ate*, I shall see you again soon," says *Bulan*.

"Yes, it's a promise," says Mala, waving goodbye.

Sidapa gives us a nod. The two make their way into the darkness of the black portal. It turns into black moths and disappears.

Then, from the shores of the Enchanted Lake, the three *Naga Sisters* emerge.

"My sisters! Hydrophis, Oligodon, Samar," *Bakunawa* says as they come around to hug her.

"We are so happy to see you back to your grace and beauty. The Mask of Gold looks beautiful on you," says Hydrophis.

"You must come back home to the Eternal Graves," says Samar.

"We must celebrate. A return of our great *Naga* sister!" says Oligodon triumphantly.

Bakunawa turns around to look toward me and Mala, "Now I must go, champions of *Zambo*," she says.

"Where will you go?" I say.

"The first thing I must do is to hide this disastrous dagger away from the likes of humanity," she says, holding onto the Serpent's Dagger, "I will put it in the Eternal Grave. Today, the Moon Eater has died, and this dagger shall be sealed away with it in the Sanctum of Secrets. I am reborn as *Bakunawa*, Deity of Eclipses, Goddess of New Beginnings," she says.

"Goddess of New Beginnings—it suits you," says Mala.

"But before I leave, please heed my warning. The Darkness—its supernatural and sinister spirit still lurks out there. I don't know where, but be careful, young heroes," she says.

"The Darkness? You mean something even more dangerous exists out there?" I say.

"It is the one that created and gave me the Serpent's Dagger and awakened my inner rage, causing me to create the lunar eclipse," says the *Bakunawa*. She bids us another farewell and returns to the depths of the Enchanted Lake's sapphire waters with her *Naga* sisters.

"A great Darkness…I have heard of such a spirit before. As a *Babaylan*, we were told the legends of the grim and forbidding nature of the spirit, but no one truly knows what the spirit is or how it came to exist," says *Ate Lanie*, "Many shamans have fallen victim to the Darkness and their black magic."

"Black magic?" asks Mala.

"Yes, shamans who manipulate the power of *lakas* to cause harm to others. They are the complete opposite of our purpose as *Babaylans*—to protect and serve the people. It makes sense that this malevolence was directly caused of such Black magic…by the Darkness. We call these sorcerers *Aswangs*,[35] those who draw power from sacrificing others for evil and selfish purposes."

"This doesn't sound good at all," I say.

Nadya pats me on my back. She raises her blade to the sky, "We shall worry about this Darkness for the future. Today, we must celebrate our victory! We must celebrate our champions who saved the *Isla Sirena*!"

"Yes, a well-earned celebration for our heroes who saved the Last Moon!" says *Ate Lanie*.

---

35 Aswang – Shamans who practice black magic; Evil spirits that take various forms

CHAPTER 15

TO NEW HOPE

Salem

We make our way back through the Forest of Lost Ones, riding slowly on the back of the Great Beast King, *Ulap*. Father and the Blood Moon Knights march back to the city with us. The knights, no longer under the spell of the *Bakunawa*, are excited to return home. I look over to Father and think of the possibilities of home, how different it will be. All this time, I held resentment. Even though it was not entirely his fault, I struggle to forgive him for deserting us, his own children. We will have to start all over again and rebuild a new life. I feel a hand lightly touch my shoulder and look up to see it is Mala's. *They must have felt my energy. My Ading understands all too well how I feel, but they have the power to forgive Father. It will just take me some time. Maybe Mala is also worried about going home. Maybe they would rather stay here, with the people of Taal and Ate Lanie. With Nadya...that sounds nice.*

When we arrive in the City of *Jati*, it is still the night of the ancient Blood Moon festival. I hear loud music and banging sounds of metal as we enter into the city. At first when we arrive, everyone stops in their tracks, in awe of

Ulap, the *Tikbalang* who ruled and dominated the forest for years. But, when they see Princess Nadya riding on his back, her bright smile and sword raised in the air, the people are no longer frightened. The people of *Taal* line the streets and parade, cheerfully banging their metal pots and pans. The musicians play their drums and flutes, dancing on every corner of the street.

At the Bamboo Palace, we hop off *Ulap* and let him rest outside. Aysha, Nami, and a few more *Taal* warriors from the kingdom surround the Blood Moon Knights to keep them from entering the palace to protect the *Lakan*, guarding him from outside. I look over to Father who just smiles and nods, "I'll be okay," he says. I give him an awkward nod and follow Nadya into the Bamboo Palace.

The festival continues within the chambers of the palace as we enter the Grand Hall.

"We have returned, Father, from the Enchanted Lake!" yells Nadya as we burst through the doors, her voice echoing into hall.

Lakan Ravi sits on his throne solemn and serious, but after seeing Nadya, his face lights up. He gets up from his throne and rushes toward us. He gives Nadya a hug. He kisses her forehead and tells her, "I am proud of you, my princess warrior, and now Tamer of the Beast King. You will make a fine *Lakan* of this kingdom someday."

"Our champions! Heroes Mala and Salem of *Zambo. Maraming Salamat!*" he cheers, "On this day, the Blood Moon Festival, we shall honor you all for your bravery in defeating the Moon Eater. The Blood Moon shall no longer symbolize the end of times, but instead new beginnings. To new hope!" *Lakan Ravi* cheers as his servants hand us cups filled with sweet-smelling wine.

"To new hope!" we toast, celebrating with the *Taal* warriors and citizens in the palace.

As the festival continues, *Lakan Ravi* asks, "So will you two be staying here on the *Isla Sirena*? We will grant you a home by the Bamboo Palace here in the City of *Jati*," he offers. I hadn't thought about staying in the Kingdom of *Taal*. *This journey is over. I wonder what life would be like to leave Zambo.* I look over to Princess Nadya, who evades my eyes. She seems saddened by the thought of us leaving. Before I can say anything, Mala says, "That won't be necessary, *Lakan Ravi*. We will be making our way back home to *Zambo* in the morning." I am surprised, *Mala wants to go back to our home—to Zambo, where the people have only ever mistreated them.*

"Mala, are you sure of this?" I ask.

They look over and nod, "Yes, I promised to return the *vinta* didn't I? Plus, the people of *Zambo* need a new *Babaylan*. *Zambo* will always be our home, *Kuya*. This time we have Father back, too. Maybe our life will be different now."

They are right. It is time for us to go home, "I will make sure that you will feel at home, *Ading*. The people of *Zambo* will respect you, our great *Babaylan* and savior of the Moon." I look over to Nadya and say, "This is not goodbye, I'll see you again."

"You better," she crosses her arms, pouting, "But I was honored to fight alongside you, Salem. You truly have the heart of a *Taal* warrior in you," she touches my heart with the palm of her hand. I blush and feel my heart flutter.

Lakan Ravi raises his hands and announces, "Then that would make Salem a fine husband for you!"

I feel embarrassed. *Husband to the princess?* I look at Nadya and find passion in her eyes. I know it will be a long time before I her face again. *I have grown to really like Nadya, her wit and strong personality. I will never meet a woman like her again.* She looks at me with a brazen face, slightly blushing, as well, and says, "Only a warrior strong enough to defeat me in battle can ever marry me."

I take a moment and give her a brazen look, too, and say, "Then it looks like I'll have to train even harder until the day I return, Princess Nadya of *Taal*."

Nadya becomes flustered at the response, her face almost bright red. I laugh at the sight and she laughs with me. *I'm going to miss her. No matter how long we will be separated, my feelings for the princess will never waver. I will come back.*

Lakan Ravi pats me on the back and raises a glass, "Now, that is the spirit of a warrior! You are a strong one, Salem of *Zambo*."

"*Ku ku ku*! Oh, to be young like you children," says *Ate Lanie*.

"*Ate Lanie*, that reminds me, the scar from the Serpent's Dagger—will you be okay?" I ask.

"Do you have access to your *lakas* power now that the *Bakunawa* has hidden the dagger and is broken away from its curse?" Mala asks.

"I'm afraid I have not gotten my special *lakas* back since the strike of that cursed dagger," she says with a disheartened face. "But worry not, my children. Remember, *lakas* energy can never be destroyed…not forever. Tomorrow, I will journey to the Tower of Kapalaran to…"

"Tower of Kapalaran?" interrupts Mala.

"Yes, the Tower of Fate. It is known by many names across different lands, but we call it the Kapalaran for its wealth, fortune, and luck. It is one of the Sacred Wonders of *lakas* in this world."

"Sacred Wonders?" I also ask.

"You're not familiar with the Sacred Wonders? The wonders are believed to be one of the first creations on Earth made by the Supreme Deity Bathala, Creator of the Universe. He left imprints of his Sacred Wonders across the parts of the world. The Enchanted Lake is one of them," explains Nadya.

"Yes, each Sacred Wonder harnesses a great source of *lakas* energy. At the Tower of Kapalaran, many shamans from all around the world visit and make pilgrimage in hopes of finding new or expanded meaning about themselves from the experiences of fortune *lakas* emitting from the tower. I hope to find my own luck in healing my *lakas* and a new personal transformation within my spirit. My people, here in *Taal,* need me as their *Babaylan*. If I am still alive, then I have to try and give it all I have got. This, I learned from you, my dear Mala and Salem of *Zambo*. Maybe one day you will visit another Sacred Wonder yourselves," *Ate Lanie* says.

"Yes, until then I will work hard to be as great a *Babaylan* like you, *Ate Lanie*," says Mala.

"You are already great, my dear. The very best! Now, let us all celebrate this auspicious evening, *ku ku ku*!" says *Ate Lanie*.

The festival goes on, and we enjoy our last night on the *Isla Sirena*.

EPILOGUE

Mala

We leave the *Isla Sirena* and sail back to our home. We ride home on the *vinta*. Salem mans the paddle and sails to lead us home, while Father quietly slumps against the side of the boat. The Blood Moon Knights follow behind us on their ships. Salem doesn't speak much on the way back; we are quiet as we try to get used to being around Father.

"We'll be reaching the ports of *Zambo* soon," says Salem, finally breaking the silence.

"You are an impressive sailor, Salem," Father musters up the energy to respond.

"Had to learn to sail to fish in order to feed Mala and I," he says, not looking at Father, busying himself with paddling the boat and manning the sail.

"Yes, Father, *Kuya* is also a really great hunter," I say, "He makes the best meals, you are going to love his cooking!"

I look at Father's drained and tired face. He is exhausted, as if the years of being under the curse of the Serpent's Dagger cost him his peace of mind.

"So much time has been lost. It's like I don't even know you both anymore," he says.

I smile at him and hold his hand. "Father, we are excited for you to get to learn about us," I tell him, "Right, *Kuya*?"

"Yes...right," Salem agrees, reluctantly.

I feel the painful energy between Salem and Father. Even within myself, I struggle to adjust. The Serpent's Dagger took Father away from us for so many years. We are victims to the effects of Black magic and the Darkness that poisoned so many at the *Bakunawa*'s growing empire. *At least we have Father back.* I touch my pearl necklace and am reminded of Mother. I know she would be happy to see our family all together again.

Father looks up to us and says, "I know no amount of apology will undo the wrong of my absence, but I want you both to know I am here now. I am not leaving your sides, not if I can help it. Salem, thank you for being the provider of the house and for taking care of your little brother when I couldn't."

"Yes, my *Ading*," Salem corrects.

"Of course, you're right. Your *Ading*," he says, smiling at me. He looks back at Salem and tells him, "Your strength and determination make you more of a man of honor than I could ever be." Then he turns his head to look back at me, "Mala, my sweet child. You are so powerful and like no other. Now, you are a *Babaylan*, too. I am so proud of you both. Your Mother would be so proud. You actually remind me of your mother, Mala. You have so much empathy and kindness, I see her magic in you."

My eyes light up. *Did I hear him right?* "Mother was magical? She was a shaman like me?" I ask.

"Yes, she was special. She had a power similar to yours. Her kindness drew me to her. She had a beautiful way of being in tune with nature and the world around us. I was always curious. She must have chosen not to become a shaman. She never told me why, but I know she would have been so excited to know you were like her, too."

I touch my necklace. *I want to learn more about Mother, and it feels so great to hear more about her from Father—to know that she, like me, could feel, manipulate, and understand the power of lakas. It makes me feel so much closer to her.* "I always feel like she is watching over Salem and me."

Finally, back at the ports of *Zambo*, we anchor the *vinta* back to its same spot on the beach. The fisherman who owned it is angry at first, so I apologized many times, bowing my head and offering to pay him. Father steps in and assures the fisherman that his *vinta* was needed for an important mission, and that because of his gracious lending of the *vinta*, he will be rewarded by the Blood Moon Knights.

"*Salamat*, Father," I say.

"I got your back this time," he says.

It is the late afternoon and the three of us walk back toward our home through the forest trail outside of the city. I missed this forest trail so much—the sound of the rivers, the songs of nature, the surrounding *lakas* of life.

Midway in the trail I realize I need to see *Lolo Alma*. "I will catch you both at home, later. I need to go visit the *Aklatan* before it closes. I have to let *Lolo Alma* know that the copperplate inscription is now back where it belongs on the Shrine of Seven Moons." *I can't wait to tell him about my entire quest.*

"Be home before dinner," says Salem.

"Be safe, Mala, see you at home," says Father. I could get used to that—Father being home with us.

The two of them head home together. *Salem needs some alone time with Father, anyways.*

As I make my way back to the city, I feel a powerful aura arrive. The *lakas* flowing are cold, but this time familiar. The signature swarm of black moths flutter around me, some of them landing on my shoulders, hands, and even on my nose.

"Hello, *Sidapa*," I say.

"Well, well, if it isn't the lunar legacy," he says as he bows to respectfully greet me. I smile at the Deity of Death, no longer fearful like our first meeting.

"Where is *Bulan*?" I ask.

"Your other brother has returned to the Moon to continue his duties. But now he can visit Earth as freely as before. He no longer needs to fear *Bakunawa*."

"That's good, I'm glad to hear he is free to see you again, too. So, what brings you back here?"

"Well, since you kept your promise to save the islands and reunite my lover back into my deathly arms, I owe our champion a repayment."

"No need for this, *Sidapa*. It was my obligation to stop the Blood Moon from ending the balance of our universe here on Earth. I was only fulfilling my role in the prophecy and legacy of *Haliya*."

"Why yes, that is true, but I do want to give you a gift. You and Salem faced many dangers together. As the Deity of Death, I would like to grant you the opportunity to speak with anyone from the Underworld through a séance."

"Anyone? I get to meet any soul that has passed?" The first and only person I think about is, "My mother." I know

Salem and Father would want a chance to see her too, even if only for today.

Sidapa approaches me and says, "I would need an object from this realm that is tethered to her soul to help me reach her and summon her spirit here." I touch my pearl necklace and unlatch it from behind my neck for the first time in years. I hand it over to *Sidapa*. "This will only be for the séance, you will have it back shortly," he says.

Sidapa clenches the pearl necklace and I feel powerful vibrations emit from his hand, as if transmitting a call. I wait. Nothing seems to have returned from his summoning.

"That is odd. It seems your Mother's spirit doesn't exist in the Underworld realm," he says.

"That can't be true—are you saying she is alive?"

"The afterlife is tricky because existence after death can take many forms. A soul that has passed could come to the Underworld and reside in my domain or they could be reborn. Your Mother's spirit is not in my realm, so she was either reborn or is still alive." *Sidapa* places the necklace in my hand, and I latch it back around my neck. I touch Mother's pearl necklace and take a deep breath. *Rebirth, just like Haliya. Or maybe she is alive!* I can't believe it. After all this time, her spirit is still here, in this realm. *Did she abandon us, too? No, I refuse to believe that. There must have been a reason. A reason like Father's. I have to find her.*

"*Salamat, Sidapa*, thank you for trying," I say. I still can't wrap my head around it. I wonder how Salem and Father would feel knowing Mother is alive.

"Is there anyone else you might like to see?" he asks.

I take a moment to think. Then it hits me. "Actually, yes, there is someone else I would like to call over. She is someone you know, actually."

I arrive at the *Aklatan* and feel the magnificent atmosphere of the archives.

I see *Lolo Alma* stocking the shelves with collections of texts. His hand is on his chin, so focused on the documents that he does not notice I have come inside.

"*Lolo Alma!*" I call to him.

"Mala!" he says, surprised, "Why, I haven't seen you in the *Aklatan* in a few days. I was worried and wondered where you had gone. Were you able to find a *Babaylan* to help you figure out your dream?"

"Yes, Lolo, I did. I travelled to a far-off island—The *Isla Sirena!* I have a story to tell that beats all the fantasy readings in the archives," I say boldly.

"I'm happy to hear that. I love stories and would love to hear of your travels, *Anak*," he says.

"But before I do, I have a *pasalubong* for you,[36] a gift from my travels."

"Oh, *Anak*, you are so sweet, what did your bring me?"

"Not a what, but a whom," I correct him.

He makes a puzzled face at me. A woman appears behind me. She slowly walks to my side, appearing in front of *Lolo Alma*. She is younger than he but still looks mature. She has short dark hair, warm brown skin, and a colorful beaded robe dress that covers her body, from the wrists of her arms to the ankles of her feet. She has a kind and open smile as she looks deeply at him, "Hello, again, my dear friend," she says.

---

36 Pasalubong – Tradition of bringing a gift from travels back home

Lolo Alma drops the texts from his hands to the floor and his glasses become crooked from his shocked face. He shakes his head and fixes his glasses, his eyes widening, "Lau!" he yells.

"It is nice to see you again. You look older now," she giggles, "But in a good way."

"You look…well the same as when I last saw you," he says in disbelief. *Lolo Alma* approaches Lau and tries to give her a hug, but his arms move through her.

"I'm sorry my old friend. I am only here as a spirit temporarily. This young *Babaylan* has brought me back from the Underworld for a séance to see you again just for today," she says.

"*Babaylan*?" *Lolo Alma* says shocked looking at me.

"Yes, it turns out that I am just like Lau, a shaman in the making. I hope to fill her shoes as best as I can to serve the City of *Zambo*," I say.

"But what about the Blood Moon Knights? It's too dangerous! We have to keep your identity a secret," he says, suddenly concerned.

"You won't have to worry about the knights anymore, Lolo. They no longer follow a code of violence. I know you have many questions, and I can't wait to tell you all about my adventure, but for now I think you should enjoy your time with Lau," I say, smiling.

Lolo Alma nods and a gives me a warm hug. "*Salamat, Anak*, I am so thankful for this gracious gift. You have given me a second chance to properly say my goodbyes to my dear friend." He then turns to Lau and says, "Please, could I have the honor to spend one final night with you before your return to the After Life?"

"Why of course, *Alma*," she chuckles.

"What would you like for us to do, Lau?" he asks.

"Read me stories from your writings, like you used to do. I always loved to hear them."

"Of course my dear friend. Anything for you," he says. The two proceed to walk down the halls of the archives together.

"That was very sweet of you," said a voice from behind me. I turn around to face *Sidapa*.

"*Lolo Alma* was my first and only friend here in *Zambo*. He gave me the copperplate inscription that Lau used to own. And throughout his time, he has dedicated his entire life to protecting our history and culture, here, as the Keeper of the *Aklatan*. This is the least I could do for him," I say.

"I couldn't agree more. You will make a fine *Babaylan*, just like Lau and *Ate Lanie*," he says.

"*Salamat, Sidapa*," I say.

Sidapa bids me another farewell and enters his black portal, "Until we meet again, Mala of *Zambo*," his voice echoes in the air. The chilling wind blows my hair softly as he disappears back to his realm, the portal returning to a group of black moths that fly into the halls of the archives. One of them lands on the palm of my hand. I look at the moth and smile.

Until we meet again.

ACKNOWLEDGMENTS

———

Maraming Salamat to everyone who has been a huge part of this journey. I still can't believe how many people it took to publish this book. I just want to give love and thanks to everyone involved in helping to bring Mala and Salem's story to life.

Thank you, Eric Koester, for giving me ten minutes of your time on the phone while I was at a coffee shop, studying for midterms, and convincing me to start this author journey. Thank you, Brian Bies, my publisher at New Degree Press, for your amazing support throughout this entire process. Thank you to Kristin Gustafson, my marketing and revisions editor, who worked with me so closely on my writing, inspired me to get lost in the magic, and encouraged me every step and page of the way. Thank you to Alexander Pyles, my developmental editor, who taught me to not let imposter syndrome stop me from trying.

Michelle Chmielowiec, you were the first person I told about this book, and I remember looking at you dead in the eyes and asking you, "Should I do it?"

You laughed and said, "What can't you do?" And so, I did. Thank you, my love.

And thank you to everyone who gave their time, donations, pre-ordered the book, helped spread the word about *Mala & the Mask of Gold* to gather amazing momentum, and helped me publish a book of which I am so proud. The countless zoom and phone calls, emails, and direct messages of support, feedback, and excitement all kept me going. I am sincerely grateful for all your help. This dream wouldn't have been a reality without you.

Josephine Badman
Lola Janet Ko
Grandma Frances & Granda
Dane Badman
Tita Leliz and Cousin Jim &
Gillian Atilano, and Lau Lau
Yaya Lanie Egoc
Robert Badman
Kuya Patrick Ko
Lolo Bong Ko
Tita Joanna &
Tito Joel Freedman
Tita Brenda Brody &
Bella Gleim
Uncle Bryan &
Aunt Robyn Badman
Aunt Kathy Badman
Uncle Tom &
Aunt Louise Greene
Aunt Pat & Uncle Gary
Rosenbloom
Cousin Max Rosenbloom
Lolo June Aguas

Jason Aguas
Lola Evelyn Han
Cousin Francesca Araneta
Cousin Ezza De La Cruz
Tita Pureza Lacaya Adasa
Alexis Beale
Giselle Cunanan
Joey Ward
Calvin A Johnson
Michelle Weinfeld
Nnamdi Nwaezeapu
Rabia Dhanani
Priya Rana
Andre Nepomuceno
Kaitlyn Yeo
Tita Elizabeth Lim Yeo
Elana Katzen
Eleanna Santos
Zoya Shaik
Sadhana Tadepalli
Karisma Magsakay
Billy Huynh
Thatyana Olivera

Vivian Truong
Tita Irene Wong
Ronelle Bautista
Justin Nwosu
Lintta Feleke-Eshete
Deena Shariq
Jordan Tisaranni
Mariah Williams
Eve Moten
Dr. Michelle Le
Betel Mekonnen
Emily Jia
Uncle Mike Lee
Tita Jeanette Acker
Tita Marichu Macrohon
Laura Torres
Jackie Liu
Mya Robinson
Sophie Whit
Nash Persaud
Kristine Pham
Leah Show-Wright
Christina Le
Robbie Hogans
Cecey Karoki
The David Sisters
(Payton & Haley)
Ayodele Akiwumi
Mozart Lalanne
Morgan Grizzle
Shige Sakurai
Celina Thomas

Yasmeen Brooks
Eileen Zheng
Kayla Cwiek
Simone Lamont
Mrinalini Nagarajan
Carter Griffin
Linda Washington
David Cáceres
Sheka Kanu
Tita Ehmy Quilloy
Kayla Creavalle
Sylvana Aho
Annie Bao
Tita Pembi Zapata
Tita Rachel Madrigal
Lena Jiao
Allyson Gower
Phil Willis
Anna Dieme
Roxanna Kazemzadeh
Eric Koester
The Chmielowiec Family
(Michelle, Sarah, & Lorie)
Patrick Driscoll
Rehan Staton
Nora Hasan
Maramae-Anne Canubas
Caitlyn Terry
Nile Fossett
Kuya Christian Flores
Cyrus Belsoi
Summer James

Whitney Clarke
Akeem Oman Cinque
Allison Aragon
Jimik Smith
Nick Schmitz
Courtney McLin
Alysa Conway
Marti Green
Dhruv Mathur
Sarah Elgendy
Uncle Barry Freedman
Alex Martinez
Olivier Ambush
Rolane Qian
Helen Serafino-Agar
Sneha Raj
Samantha Beitzell
Priyanka and
Pritika Kishore
Corinne Baker
Rhea Caplan
Tita Anabelle Casero
Tita Lorna Calabon
Gabriela Pena
Dorothy Lee
Tita Jennifer Clark
Makaile Bishop
Ryan Holt
Aimee Brennan
Thaddeus Lee-Tyson
Ryan Brand

Kevin Ninh
(aka Flawless Kevin)
dadinaro2
Ted Sauerland
Taylor Bailey
Ate Nessa Rillorta
Lexi Opdenaker
Ate Janeva Duran
Tita Mary Shobee Ko
Velasquez-Horvath
Jillian McGuffey
Tita Caroline Gonzales
Ate Katie Medina
Ate Noemi Arquero
Andrew Saundry
Shelton Daal
Brandon Elliott
Stacey Audrey Mannuel
Sara Cha
Elmer Jonathan Garcia
Taylor Mathis
Cousin Kenny Sicat
Numrah Shaikh
Thuy-Giang Caitlin Le
Karina Absalon
Auntie Edna Brunner
Uncle Leo Brunner
Cousin Kyle Ko
Lola Fely Yanga
Lolo Rogelio Yanga
Cousin Sheena Shine

Jordyn Perez Pugh
Mifrah Baqai
Hannah Shraim
Tingwei Hsu
Skye Knight
Sadie Inez West
Tito Ron Domingo & Tita
Regina Domingo
Justyn Alexander
Doyin Oladimeji-Stevens
Tita Vida T. Daria
Alexis Doryumu
Tita Alejandra Alberto

Lester Echem and
Arya Echem
Kayla Marie Louise Chan
Tita Mylene Chan
Brittany Tabora
Lydia Parker
Hunter Petit
Margot Trouve
Alon Sherman
Tita Claudine Coffin
Victoria Atkinson
Alawi Masud
Dean Victor Mullins

It takes a village. And with you all, I had the courage to publish my book.

If you'd like to learn more about Filipino/a/x mythology: *Please check out the Aswang Project—an educational resource that was created to share the rich and diverse cultures, mythology, and folklore of the Philippines.*

I'd like to acknowledge a few sources of inspiration: *Rick Riordan, James Baldwin, Michael Dante DiMartino, Bryan Konietzko, Yoshihiro Togashi, and Mom.*

Lastly, I'd like to thank you, dear reader, for taking a chance on this book and joining Mala and Salem on this quest. May the Deities foresee many more quests for these two to come—or, for Mala, another encounter with black moths perhaps?

Thank you for joining our magical family; I hope you found your inner *lakas,* making you the hero of your own story, too.

Art of *Mala and Salem* illustrated by the wonderful Kayla Creavalle–Kingkanny.com

CITATIONS

Arrows free icon. This cover has been designed using resources from Flaticon.com. Icon made by Freepik from www.Flaticon.com

Freepik, "Arrows free icon," *Flaticon*. Retrieved from https://www.flaticon.com/free-icon/arrows_96419?term =archery%20bow&page=1&position=96

Crescent Moon Phase Shape with Two Stars free icon. This cover has been designed using resources from Flaticon. com. Icon made by Freepik from www.Flaticon.com

Freepik, "Crescent Moon Phase Shape with Two Stars free icon," *Flaticon*. Retrieved from https://www.flaticon.com/ free-icon/crescent-moon-phase-shape-with-two-stars_4201 1?term=moon&page=1&position=35

GLOSSARY

abyan—Spirit guide; companion to *Babaylans*

ading—Younger sibling

Anak—Child

Aswang—Shamans who practice black magic; Evil spirits that take various forms

ate (ah-teh)—Older sister

Babaylan—Shaman, spiritual practitioners of the pre-colonial Philippine islands

Bakunawa—Deity of Eclipses; Moon Eater; Great Serpent; Creator of the Lunar Eclipse

bakyas—Wooden clogs; Traditional footwear

barong—Embroidered long sleeved traditional garment

Baybayin—Ancient writing script of the pre-colonial Philippines

bukaw—Eagle-owl endemic to the Philippines

Bulan—One of the Seven Moon Deities; The Last Moon

Datu—Chief of City or Village

Engkantos—Fairies or mythical spirits

golok—Broadsword machete

Haliya—One of the Seven Moon Deities; The Golden Moon

Kaluwalhatian—World of Glory; Realm above the skies; the heavens

Kuya—Older Brother

Lakan—Paramount ruler; equivalent to Rajah or King

Lakapati—Deity of Fertility & Agriculture; known for her kindness amongst all the other Deities; Transgender Deity and protector of fields

lakas—"Strength" in Tagalog; it is the spiritual/magical energy, power, lifeforce of this world

latigo—Long whip

Lolo—Grandfather; elder

Malaya—Freedom

Manananggal—Malevolent, man-eating and blood-sucking monster native to the Philippines

Maraming Salamat—Thank you very much

Nagas—Water spirits; sea serpent deities that guard the gates of the Underworld; Keepers of treasure, wealth and secrets of the dead

pana—Traditional wooden bow

pasalubong—Tradition of bringing a gift from travels back home

Salamat—Thank you

sibat—Spear

Sidapa— Deity of Death, King of the Underworld

Takay Flowers Purple water hyacinth; gift from the lunar deity; legend is native to the Bicolano people

Tala—Deity of the Stars

tameng—Shield

Tikbalang—Bipedal horse creature that dwells in mountains and forests; native to the Philippines; Beast King; Keeper of the Forest of Lost Ones

vinta—Traditional outrigger board made by the local *Zambo* peoples living in the archipelago; based on Philippine island of Mindanao